A Scions of Belhaven novella

BOUND BY INK

Ariella Monti

sweet
magnolia
media

Cover Design: Amanda Hawkins, Eternal Geekery Design
Editing: Jenny Sliger, Owl Eyes Proofs and Edits
Diversity Consultant: Ruthie Bowles, No Market for That Book

First edition 2026
Paperback ISBN 979-8-9920601-9-5
eBook ISBN 979-8-9943046-0-0

Series: Scions of Belhaven
Reading order: 2nd
Adult Fiction – Romance – Fantasy

To the mothers that came before:
May we hold your wisdom close so that we may never
repeat your mistakes.

BEFORE WE GET STARTED

Content advisory

Bound by Ink is a fantasy romance set in a fictional world that is similar to our own. While it has a happy ending, this book contains dark themes, discussions, and events. It is not intended for readers under 18 and contains the following elements:

Terminal illness
Death
Severe mental illness and depressive episodes
Explicit sexual intimacy
Intimate partner violence (verbal)
Imprisonment
Parental abandonment
Explicit language
Ritualistic self-harm
Physical violence

Reading order

While the events of *Bound by Ink* happen in the past, it is best appreciated when read after finishing *Roots in Ink*.

I didn't write *Roots in Ink* with Sara and Bethany's story in mind. It wasn't until I was done with Emma and Liam's story that I knew Sara and Bethany's needed to be told.

I hadn't planned on publishing it next. I was already drafting the second novel in the Scions of Belhaven series. But after the 2024 presidential election and subsequent inauguration, I felt compelled to get this sapphic story in reader hands while I was still legally able.

Working backwards proved to be a much bigger challenge than I anticipated. With *Roots in Ink* already out in the world, I had to work under a set of constraints entirely of my own making. My characters didn't always want to adhere to those constraints, which is not something I experience very often.

I drove myself a bit crazy trying to keep *Bound by Ink* consistent with *Roots in Ink* and I hope you can forgive anything that slipped by me.

Mental Illness and Intimate Partner Violence

Bound by Ink is a fictional story about imaginary people who live in a magical world that doesn't exist . But it deals with the very real challenges of mental illness and touches on intimate partner violence.

You are real and you exist.

If you're struggling with depression, emotional distress, alcohol or drug use, or just need to talk to someone, please reach out to the suicide and crisis lifeline at 988 or 988lifeline.org/.

You deserve to be in a healthy relationship. If you aren't and you need assistance, contact the National Domestic Violence Hotline at 1.800.799.SAFE (7233) or visit thehotline.org/get-help/

Chapter I

Sara

A violent crack of lightning overhead sent a pulse of energy through the forest, rattling both Sara Cortese's magic and her nerves. Her drenched cloak did little to protect her from the rain; nonetheless, she pulled it tightly around her and continued her journey to the forests of Belhaven's northern coast.

Only a summons from Maryanne Banner would bring Sara out in this kind of weather. An incurable illness struck her friend and mentor, and it was only a matter of time before Maryanne left this earthly plane to join the Amora Goddesses in their celestial home of Terultimi.

The slippery trail Sara followed through the forest brought her to a wide dirt path flattened by wagon wheels and heavy livestock feet. At the end of the road stood the log cabin that Maryanne shared with her wife Eliza. Dry-stone structures served as shelters for the myriads of animals Maryanne cared for as an animal keeper.

Through the blur of the pelting rain, Sara made out a small herd of onyx unicorns standing vigil at the edge of the tree line. They seemed unbothered by the storm, but as Sara approached, they shifted warily on their long legs, unsure if Sara was friend or foe. Somewhere in the trees, a chickadee sang a reassuring tune, and the unicorns settled back into stillness.

Eliza opened the door just as Sara reached the garden gate.

"Watch out for the puddle below the step, dear! It's deeper than it looks!" Eliza yelled over the rain.

Sara heeded the older woman's warning and leapt over the pooled rainwater, onto the landing, and stumbled through the threshold.

"The twilight hens have taken to using that spot for their dust baths," Eliza said as she peeled the cloak from Sara's body and hung it near the glowing fire at the other end of the room.

"I thought they preferred the trees." Sara bent over to unbuckle her boots. Her feet were cold but dry, and she thanked the Goddesses and her neighbor Lerato's skilled leatherwork.

"They've been hanging around a bit more closely since Maryanne became ill." Eliza took Sara's boots and rested them near her cloak. "I think they know she'll be traveling through their realm soon and may accompany her."

"That explains the unicorns," Sara said, moved by their show of grief for their keeper. She released a slow breath to keep her tears at bay.

"I'll care for them as best I can when she's gone, but without the bonds of keeper magic, I can only do so much," Eliza said solemnly.

Sara's already broken heart broke further for Eliza. She was losing the love of her life and the person that made much of their work possible. The lives of humans and the forest creatures of their world, Tereprima, were so intertwined that bonds were easily formed regardless of a person's magical lineage. But the mystical animals that visit from Teremedi, the plane between theirs and the celestial lands of the Amora Goddesses, were far less trusting without the kind of magic Maryanne was born with.

These things weren't set in stone, however. "Maryanne isn't the only animal keeper on the island, but you've been beside her for so long that I'm confident you've earned their trust," Sara reasoned.

She finally removed the small satchel strapped across her chest and handed it to Eliza.

"Give Maryanne three drops from the vial as she falls asleep to keep the nightmares at bay," Sara instructed. "I can't say for certain how well it will work, but the spell itself is harmless."

Eliza's full lips curled into a warm smile even as her dark brown eyes became glassy with unshed tears. Holding the satchel close to her chest, Eliza gently grasped Sara's hand. Sara's hands were still cold from her journey, and the older woman's copper-brown skin was warm and soft against hers.

"You're the most talented herbal alchemist of your generation, Sara Cortese. You need to have more confidence in your work."

Unable to take the compliment, Sara looked away and tried to smooth her chestnut-brown hair. The rain turned her tight waves into haphazard curls that escaped her long braid.

Eliza stepped away to make a fresh pot of Sara's tea. The hem of Sara's too-long trousers dragged over the floor as she padded into Maryanne's room.

Maryanne Banner was not one for rest and seeing her in bed in the middle of the day was a disconcerting sight. Even when she dozed after a long night caring for nocturnal animals, Maryanne's body still found a way to move. Tossing and turning to the point that Eliza slept in a separate bed. In all the time Sara had known her, no illness had ever stilled Maryanne like this.

Sara sat in the chair squeezed between the two beds. Maryanne's usually fair skin had a yellow pallor, and the lines around her light brown eyes had deepened. Eliza had pinned back Maryanne's short white hair and tied a scarf around it. In only a few short weeks, Maryanne looked like she aged over a decade well past her seventieth year.

A gray ball of fur nestled in the bend of Maryanne's neck and shoulder belonged to Willow, a chunky gray squirrel. Under a fluffy tail, Sara found a sleepy squirrel head and gave it a little scratch between the ears.

"Look in on Eliza after I leave," Maryanne said quietly. Her heavy eyelids struggled to open.

"Are you talking to me or Willow?" Sara smiled and took her friend's hand. Her skin was cold to the touch and rough like old pine bark.

"Both." A weak smile appeared on Maryanne's face.

"You know I will." Sara laughed through her nose. "Does that mean Willow won't be joining you on your journey?"

Maryanne's magic allowed her to have special connections with nonhuman creations, but the Goddesses sent Willow to her when she most needed a guide. These animal companions lived alongside their humans, well past their natural lifespan, so they could journey to Terultimi together. But sometimes, they stayed behind.

"No, but I'll look forward to seeing her when she comes with Eliza."

Maryanne's smile disappeared, and her face turned serious. "The elders will call upon you to take my place as lore keeper."

As village scribe and keeper of lore, Maryanne was tasked with recording meetings of the Council of Nine and the day-to-day lives of Amora who lived on the Isle of Belhaven.

"And I will accept it as we always intended," Sara confirmed.

They'd discussed this transition before, but Sara hadn't anticipated filling the position so soon. This kind of recordkeeping was an important part of the Amoran culture, and Sara felt like she still had far too much to learn. Where other cultures disappeared from existence, the Amora, their traditions, and their magic remained alive for thousands of years. Sara didn't feel quite ready for that kind of trust.

Maryanne squeezed Sara's hand with unexpected urgency. "Sara, your responsibility will be to the elders, but you are swearing your oath to the Amora of this island. Your truth will be of great importance to our descendants."

Taken aback by the older woman's warning, Sara silently nodded her head.

"You must continue to keep your own journals just like I taught you." Maryanne's eyes briefly came alive, and Sara couldn't look away. "Keep them separate and keep them hidden."

Sara's own deep hazel eyes narrowed in confusion. "Why separate? Why hidden?"

Maryanne sighed a laugh. "Because there will always be those in power who are threatened by the accurate recording of history."

Chapter 2

Bethany

The last remaining rays of sunlight rippled over the sea, catching the gentle waves and riding them to shore. Healing doula Bethany Clement spent much of her life watching these sunsets from her home in Willow Ridge, a small but bustling port city on the Arcanos mainland south of Belhaven. Standing on the island's shores offered her a new and unique perspective, perfect for the communal ritual she was attending.

Belhaven's Amora bustled around her for the Feast of the Spring Moon, their eyes glancing at the sky in wait of the rising full moon. It was Bethany's favorite seasonal celebration. Though the timing was purely coincidental, she thought it appropriate that her first days in Belhaven as its healing doula would coincide with a ritual to celebrate growth and new beginnings.

She used some kindling to carefully light the candle cradled in her hand while she gave thanks to the lunar Goddesses for the restful darkness of winter. Bethany placed the candle among the offerings: animal pelts, woven blankets, smoked meats, horseshoes, jewelry. As a healer, she didn't have tangible abundance to share with the members of her new community. But the lighting of her candle was in memory of those who passed, in gratitude of those who lived, and a promise to care for herself and the people of her village.

A faint but harsh buzz of anxious energy crawled over Bethany's skin. It was a gentle reminder to keep her magic close so she wouldn't be overwhelmed by the auras around her. Once she got to know them, the gentle hum of her magic connecting with others would bring comfort and live harmlessly in the air around her, but until then, she needed to exert more control.

The source of the unsettling energy was the daughter of Bethany's primary patient, John Dawson. Even prior to John's illness, Piper Dawson, as the oldest daughter, was responsible for the lion's share of the metalwork her family did for the village. At fifteen, she took over for her mother Rebekah, allowing her to focus on schooling and training the younger children. By twenty-three, she had taken on the most labor-intensive tasks. Caring for a sick parent added a layer of exhaustion and worry.

Despite the anxiety, Piper approached Bethany with a lightness in her step that almost seemed at odds with her tall, muscular frame. Metalwork had given her beautifully strong arms and legs that moved with soft and subtle grace. The rose undertones in her light brown skin absorbed the nearby candlelight, giving her an incandescent glow.

"Try this." Piper placed a lumpy cookie in Bethany's open palm.

"It's made with eggs from Twilight Hens," Piper added before Bethany could ask.

Bethany marveled at the dessert. It looked completely ordinary and unremarkable, but its ingredients were incredibly rare. "But they never lay eggs in this realm."

"It doesn't happen often, that's for sure," Piper said with her mouth full.

"Where did these come from then?" Bethany slowly broke the pastry in half, admiring the texture.

"Eliza Banner made them," Piper explained. "Her late partner Maryanne was one of our animal keepers, and the hens laid a large clutch before she died. Maryanne said the eggs were a gift Eliza could use to make her favorite cookies. They keep even longer than earthbound hens, and Eliza had plenty left over to make enough for tonight."

Bethany hadn't met Eliza yet, but a bloom of appreciation for the woman rose in her chest. She felt incredibly lucky to be there at a time to receive such a meaningful offering.

"That's ..." she trailed off, the cookie inches from her lips. Her eyes landed on a woman on the other side of the large offering table. "... beautiful."

The dessert never made it to her mouth because the stunning woman had Bethany in her grasp without so much as a glance in her direction.

This mysterious woman admired the offerings piled on the table, rocking in that way mothers do because the movement remains etched in their muscles. With every sway, a gemstone in the hilt of a dagger strapped to her full hips glinted in the waning light.

She twirled a lock of her long, chestnut-brown hair while the rest flowed in tight waves down her back, skimming the valleys of her waist. The skirt of her scarlet dress fluttered in the sea breeze. A deep orange bodice covered in embroidered flowers enhanced the curves of her breasts and hips. The autumn colors of her clothes complemented the warm tones in her light skin.

Bethany was mesmerized.

"Oh! There's Sara!" Piper exclaimed.

"Who?" Bethany was shocked out of her hypnosis and finally took a bite of the precious cookie melting in her hand.

"Sara Cortese. The herbal alchemist I wanted you to work with."

Piper grabbed Bethany's other hand and pulled her around the table toward the stunning creature. Bethany pocketed the rest of the treat in time for Piper to present her to an earthbound goddess.

"Lunar blessings, Sara!" Piper cheered.

Sara returned the greeting with a wide smile.

Now closer, Bethany saw that Sara's hair was pinned away from her face with combs adorned with gemstones that sparkled like stars against the dark sky. The firelight brought out the deep green in her hazel eyes, which were lightly lined with kohl. Her lips were the pink of raspberries, and her teeth were slightly crooked as though they healed improperly after an injury and created a charmingly beautiful smile. A smile that likely happened often given the delicate lines around her eyes and mouth.

"Sara, this is Bethany Clement," Piper introduced. Bethany was grateful that Piper was taking the lead because Bethany's words failed to materialize. "She's the healing doula sent by the Willow Ridge elders."

"Lunar blessings, Bethany. Welcome to Belhaven," Sara said softly, shifting on her feet like she wanted to welcome her with a hug, but quickly reconsidered.

Bethany now yearned for Sara's embrace, feeling an emptiness without it.

"My father is her first charge," Piper continued. "And she asked to work with the herbal alchemist that I trusted most."

"And that's me?" Sara brought her hands to her heart as though she were preventing it from bursting through her chest. Her face melted into a mix of joy and embarrassment.

It must be you! Bethany wanted to scream.

Despite Bethany's control of her magic, it sought out Sara's, and the energies twisted together like young woodbine.

"Of course it's you!" Piper screamed instead. A few villagers turned toward the sound before shaking their heads with a chuckle. "You've always been like an older sister to me."

Piper turned to Bethany. "My cycles were horrendous when I was a child. Sara was at my bedside every month, delivering something to help with the pain and the bleeding. She always stayed a while to keep me company and distract me while her potions took effect."

"Piper had the best village gossip." Sara winked. "Well, you've made me quite emotional with your request. Of course I'll help Bethany care for your father. We'll do everything we can to get him well."

Bethany tried to hide her elation behind a tempered smile. "Wonderful," she squeaked, then made a show of clearing her throat.

Sara wasn't the first herbal alchemist that Bethany found attractive, but Bethany knew from that moment Sara was the first she'd fall in love with.

Chapter 3
Sara

When Sara arrived at the Dawson home, she found Bethany in the kitchen, slouched over a steaming cup of tea. The pair had been working together for half a moon cycle, and John's illness only seemed to progress. The frustration was starting to chip away at them both.

"I'm sorry I didn't get here sooner," Sara said. "I planned on riding today, but Zephyr was having a stubborn morning."

Bethany gave a weak laugh but didn't look up. She raked her fingers through her golden-brown curls in a repetitive motion that increased when Bethany was tired. Dark purple circles accompanied a dullness in her emerald eyes, and her light skin lacked the delicate pink in her cheeks.

"You look exhausted," said Sara.

And still so beautiful, she thought.

"That's good considering I feel like death."

Sara rubbed Bethany's back the way she did when her children felt the same. After a few gentle circles, Bethany's tense body loosened, and her hands fell away from her head and around her cup.

Sara fingered Bethany's soft curls, twirling them loosely to reshape them into ringlets. She should have asked first, but at the same moment she realized she didn't have Bethany's permission, Bethany leaned back into the chair, taking her tea with her. In between sips, she closed her eyes and tipped her head, following Sara's movements. Sara had only known Bethany for a short time, but she learned quickly that Bethany Clement didn't do anything she didn't want to do.

Pulling a scarf from her pocket, Sara began smoothing Bethany's hair away from her face, creating more ringlets as she went.

"John's body is filled with so much pain," Bethany said, her eyes still closed. "And it's hard for me to get beyond the pain to whatever is causing it. It's especially draining. I don't usually feel this kind of . . . emptiness."

"What are you looking for?" Sara finished wrapping Bethany's hair in the scarf and sat down.

"Something stronger to ease his headaches. If we can bring the severity of his headaches down, then it may be easier for me to target my magic to whatever is causing the headaches."

Sara pulled her journal out of her satchel and quickly flipped the pages until she found an index of spring plants.

"And something that could also help him sleep and slow his heartbeat," Bethany added. "It's racing constantly."

Her mind percolated, the thoughts bubbling, but not yet fully formed. Sara closed her book and put it back in her satchel. "I have some ideas. I'll need to collect a few things. I won't be long."

Sara left and wandered into the forest to find blooms from trailing arbutus and blue toadflax, ripe scarlet strawberries, young stems of woodbine, bark shavings and leaves from a sassafras tree, and the needles from a pignut hickory.

It was tempting to take her time. Every day, it grew harder being around John. Stepping into his room was stepping into a cloud of misery. But she couldn't leave Bethany.

Sara's maternal line was gifted this magic by the Amora Goddesses. Her mother trained her to do this work. Now Sara's children were learning the craft. One day, they might assist a healing doula in caring for their community.

But it was so much more than responsibility.

If being around John was like stepping into a cloud of misery, being with Bethany was the sun on Sara's face.

Hot. Bright. Invigorating.

She soaked it in like a seedling breaking through the soil and reaching for light.

It wasn't just that she couldn't leave Bethany, it was also that she didn't want to. She was a teenager the last time she felt pulled to a person in this way. Now, Sara found herself in her thirty-fifth year feeling the same kind of infatuated giddiness.

With only a few distractions delaying her (a true testament to Bethany's influence), Sara returned to the Dawson home with her ingredients.

"How can I help?" Bethany asked, shutting the door to John's room behind her.

"Take that cup of tea," Sara instructed with utmost seriousness.

Bethany picked it up with fatigued eagerness.

"And now go outside and touch the grass."

Bethany pursed her lips, slight annoyance playing on her face, making Sara laugh.

"You said it yourself. You feel empty. Connect with the earth, replenish your well of magic, and then *maybe* I'll let you help me."

"Ugh," Bethany groaned and rolled her eyes. "Fine."

Sara laughed even harder as Bethany huffed through the kitchen on her way outside.

Humming a long-unsung lullaby to keep her focus, Sara separated the buds and leaves from the stems and chopped them into fine pieces. They went into her mortar along with a handful of scarlet strawberries and sassafras shavings. The tiny berries popped under the weight of the pestle and mixed with the rich aroma of the sassafras bark.

The tingling of Sara's magic flowed from her chest to her fingertips, in search of the goodness held within each plant's veins and cells. Once thoroughly mashed, she scooped the mixture into her hands and held it over the simmering water. She whispered an incantation, and her hands warmed with her magic's invisible glow. The mixture went into the pot to join the waiting woodbine stems and hickory needles.

Sara was inspecting the brew when Bethany rejoined her. The delicate pink had returned to the woman's cheeks, and her emerald-green eyes glowed brighter. The bounce returned to Bethany's step, and she stood a bit taller.

"Now how can I help?" Bethany asked, leaning against the worktable.

"Thank you for asking, but I'm all finished," Sara said, taking the pot off the fire.

Bethany put her hands on her hips, but her indignation failed to manifest. "Tricky wench."

Sara stuck her tongue out in a show of immaturity that matched the lightness Bethany brought out of her. "Would you like to ladle some into a cup so that it cools more quickly?"

"Yes, I would." Bethany's smile defied the firm tone.

Sara stepped aside and let Bethany fill a teacup with a ladle of the bucolic liquid. "Do you feel better now?"

"Yes. Yes, I do."

John Dawson sat in a dark room save for a sliver of sunlight breaking through the drawn curtains. When Sara and Bethany approached, he was pressing his fingers into his temples, his eyes squeezed shut, and his jaw clenched.

Sara came by almost every day, and every day it was a shock to see the changes in her friend's body and mind. John's light brown skin was similar in color to Piper's, but illness had stripped it of its soft glow. His once strong, thick hands seemed to vanish overnight, leaving frail fingers in their place. John had been a large man in height and build, but as his body thinned and his back rounded, he appeared to shrink to half his size.

He startled when Bethany touched his arm, but relief quickly replaced the initial fear in his cloudy gray eyes.

"Hello John," Sara said, keeping her voice just above a whisper. "I have something new for the pain."

"About damn time," he mumbled, taking the cup with trembling hands.

Sara nearly scolded John like he was one of her children, but she let it go. He wasn't usually so ornery and clearly felt miserable.

Bethany supported the cup as he brought it to his lips and drank. When the last drop was gone, Bethany handed it back to Sara.

"Well?" Bethany prodded.

"It was disgusting so I imagine it will be quite effective," John forced a smile. His lips were dry and cracked, and Sara made a mental note to bring a thicker lotion.

"That's usually how it goes," Sara replied.

John took a deep breath and let it out slowly. "I do believe it's working to take the edge off the pain. Thank you. Apologies for my tone. That was uncalled for."

Sara waved him off. "I hope the relief is sustained. I should go home and get started on turning this into an elixir."

"I'll walk you out," Bethany offered.

The women stepped outside into the fresh spring air. The late midday sun broke through the trees and warmed the landing in front of the door.

"Thank you for your support today," Bethany said.

"Of course. I'll come by tomorrow with something more concentrated." Sara began to walk away.

"No." Bethany lunged forward and grabbed her hand, stopping Sara in her tracks and sending an explosion of heat through her core.

"I mean, yes," Bethany stammered. "Yes, thank you for John's tea and for the elixir. But I was talking about how you *saw* I was struggling and sent me outside to replenish my magic."

Sara adjusted her fingers so she could properly hold Bethany's hand. They fit together like the perfect lock and key.

"Thank you for caring for me," Bethany said.

"Of course," Sara replied, though the words couldn't harness all that she wanted to say. "I'll always care for you."

CHAPTER 4
BETHANY

Bethany intended to spend her rare afternoon off in the village tavern reading a novel Piper lovingly forced upon her, but those plans were thwarted when Catrina Boudin and Eliza Banner spotted her tucked away at her table.

She didn't mind the interruption, however. Bethany loved being around people in her community, but since most interactions happened during private and vulnerable moments, it was always a struggle for her to initiate conversation outside of those circumstances. The people of Belhaven proved to be the exception in this respect. From the start, they welcomed her like one of their own. The community bond was one of the strongest she'd ever seen from an Amoran village, and they were equally welcoming to anyone that called the island home.

When Bethany first met Eliza, she was still mourning the loss of her partner—and Sara's mentor—Maryanne. Grief would always be evident in Eliza's aura, but Bethany felt her strengthening joy. Maryanne may have been the lorekeeper of the pair, but Eliza had a flair for storytelling that kept Bethany enraptured like no other.

Catrina was a talented lapidary who always wore the most incredible pieces of art, and that afternoon Bethany peppered the woman with questions about her craft.

"I haven't worn jewelry like this in ages." Bethany admired one of Catrina's gemstone bracelets. The glimmering mix of purples, pinks, and blues was a tangible sunrise Catrina got to wear on her slender wrists every day.

"My mentor told me dozens of times that I shouldn't wear jewelry, but I was young and stubborn, and she let me learn the hard way. A child—this little shit—" Bethany laughed at the memory. "Yanked my favorite necklace so hard the chain broke and sent the beads flying across the room. Never again."

She handed the bangle back to Catrina, almost sad to see it go, but it looked even better when stacked against the rest in a rainbow of colors and metals.

"Well, I'd be thrilled to make you something extravagant," Catrina said with a flourish of her dark-brown, bangled hand. "I'll even source the metal chain from Piper, so it'll be strong enough to withstand the brute strength of the shittiest child."

The women continued their lively banter as the tavern overflowed with patrons filling their bellies with food and drink before the bard's performance that evening. Bethany was saying goodbye to Eliza when she caught a glimpse of Sara's husband Stephen. He was hard to miss. Strapping was the first word that came to mind. Almost comically tall and barrel-chested with long blond hair and a beard to match. They'd met once before, only briefly, much like how she'd met most people in the village.

Stephen caught her staring and further embarrassed her by yelling hello across the tavern. He pushed through the crowd towards them, stopping to greet Eliza before she made it out the door.

"Bethany! It's so good to see you out and enjoying yourself!" Stephen said after greeting Catrina. "Sara's told me how exhausted you've been."

Bethany flushed with the revelation that she'd been a topic of conversation in the Cortese household. "Well, the elixir she concocted has made a noticeable difference in John's illness, so I really have her to thank."

Catrina excused herself to buy another round of drinks, leaving Bethany alone with Stephen.

"She'll be so happy to hear that," Stephen said. "She's been worried about you."

Bethany's skin prickled with goosebumps, and her heart thundered against her ribs. Surely it meant nothing more than concern for a friend. She had no reason to believe that Sara wasn't romantically content with the beautiful man in front of her. Despite all their time spent together, Bethany didn't know much about Sara's family life. And Sara would probably say the same about Bethany. Those were the kinds of conversations that happened in her free time, and Bethany had even less of that than usual.

"I really enjoy working with her. Sara's an extremely talented alchemist. I'm not sure she realizes how few there are of her caliber." Bethany took a sip of her remaining ale, hoping the oversized container hid the heat spreading over her cheeks.

"She speaks very highly of you as well," Stephen said. "She has a glow about her that I haven't seen since our youth."

"Oh?" Bethany uttered. "Surely you still make her heart flutter after all this time."

Stephen shook his head while he swallowed a mouthful of ale. "We are spiritually bonded as soulmates, and I love Sara deeply as the mother of my children and my closest friend, but our journey as romantic partners ended some time ago."

Bethany nodded as she processed this new information. "The Goddesses don't make mistakes when they connect our souls. But sometimes we mistake the kind of connection for which our souls were meant."

Stephen raised his tankard in agreement. "Sara and I were meant to share a life together, and I love the life we share. But there are others who are also meant to be in our lives, and we are both free to pursue finding them."

He set his tankard on the table and leaned in close. "And if you ask me, I think she's already found someone."

A mixture of emotions hit Bethany at the same time: curiosity, jealousy, excitement.

"And if I ask, would you tell me who you think it is?"

Stephen barked a laugh. "Of course not!" he cried.

But then he leaned in again, with an impish smile on his face and sincerity in his dark brown eyes. "But I think you know. You just have to be brave enough to confirm it."

Stephen left her with that, walking away to canoodle with a man and a woman on the other side of the room.

Bethany thought about the way her magic always reached for Sara when they were together. She usually had so much control over her magic, but if she were a moth, Sara was a flame.

What would she find if she let it go just a bit?

CHAPTER 5

SARA

Sara examined her artwork in the corner of a blank page in a nearly full journal. It wasn't bad considering how quickly she needed to work.

She'd been foraging in the forest on the other side of the village when she spotted nectar fairies visiting some early milkweed blooms. While watching them from a distance, Sara sketched the movements of their tiny bodies as they flew from stem to stem collecting the dusty yellow powder. They were a bit like bees, and a bit like butterflies, with vaguely human-like features.

No one was quite sure what they did with the pollen once they returned to their home in Teremedi. They were docile spirits but extremely secretive and only sought assistance from animal keepers as a last resort. Maryanne had only cared for two over her lifetime, and Sara wondered if her friend encountered them on her journey through their realm.

Her mind wandered to memories of her friend as she refined the rushed lines, adding more depth and detail to the sketch.

The sound of heavy boots outside the door caught her ear, and the whisper of Stephen's magic brushed against her skin. She set aside her journal and the book she'd been referencing, and padded to the kitchen to prepare him a cup of tea. Sara could hear the exhaustion in his clumsy movements as he came through the door. He was never light on his feet, and it worsened at the end of the day or in this case, a visit to the tavern.

"The children are asleep already?" he whispered after kissing her cheek.

"They came foraging with me but were absolutely useless because they spent the entire time in the creek." Sara smiled with the memory of their laughter.

"That'll do it," he said mid-yawn.

Suspecting Stephen had several aches and pains he'd refuse to complain about, Sara reached for a jar of balm and waved it in his face. He'd spent most of the day working on the small cabin he was building next to their family home. Stephen came from a family of woodworkers, and while the work was familiar and in his blood, it was no less tiring.

He rolled his eyes. "I'm fine." His long blond beard did little to hide the deepening wrinkles as his lips fought a smile.

Sara raised a skeptical eyebrow, and Stephen relented with a sigh, taking the jar from her and finding a seat by the fire. Inseparable as children, a lifetime together meant few words needed to be exchanged.

Carrying two cups of tea, Sara carefully made her way to where Stephen was rubbing ointment into the rough skin of his elbows and down his forearms, to his wrists. Had she not been focusing on keeping her teacups steady, Sara would have teased him about using so much ointment when he was—in his words—*fine*.

"I saw Bethany at the tavern this evening," he said, his eyes sparkling with mischief.

Sara set his cup where he could reach and settled back into her own chair. "Oh?"

Stephen ran his palms over his straw-colored hair. Just enough ointment remained on his hands to smooth the shorter strands away from his face.

"That's all you're going to say? Oh?" He laughed at full volume despite their sleeping children. "You're usually such a gossip."

Sara took a sip of tea to hide her smile. Stephen was right.

She pounced on him the moment he returned home from the tavern, wanting to know every tale, big and small. It was part of her job as the keeper of lore to know the goings-on in the village, but mostly she just loved the stories. She shared few beyond the walls of their home. Maryanne taught Sara how to discern between news worth sharing and personal matters that should remain in tight circles.

"Indulge me, husband," Sara said. Her words were coated with sass, but she genuinely wanted anything Stephen had to share about Bethany Clement.

She couldn't get the healer out of her mind, sometimes becoming so distracted Sara didn't hear the call of her own children. Now that they were older and gaining their independence, Sara enjoyed spending time with a few others in the village. Where those men and women made her stomach flutter, Bethany made Sara's heart race and left her breathless.

But Sara didn't know much about Bethany's life outside of John Dawson's home. They were together frequently to work through John's symptoms and discuss how best to ease his suffering. Rarely did those conversations delve into their own personal lives.

"Shall I give you a chance to get your journal? Would you like to take some notes?" Stephen teased.

"Get on with it, and when you're finished, I'll decide if it's worthy of the official record."

"She's especially fond of you," Stephen said. "She had the afternoon off because your elixir has been quite successful at easing John's symptoms. She said there are few herbal alchemists of your caliber."

"That's good. I enjoy working with her." Sara tried to keep her voice neutral, but Stephen knew her well and had likely picked up on the delight in her tone.

"Funny you should say that." He sat up taller in his seat and crossed an ankle over his knee as he often did when he was preparing to make some kind of point. "Because she said the same about you, and her cheeks turned just as flush."

Stephen took a loud and obnoxious sip of his tea and stared at Sara with wide, knowing eyes. Sara was utterly incapable of hiding her emotions, and Stephen always knew immediately when she had her eyes on someone. But Sara was feeling particularly petty this evening and wouldn't give her ex-lover the satisfaction of a response.

"I could tell she was curious about our familial arrangements," he continued. "I assured her that although you and I are spiritually bound as parents to our children and the closest of friends, we are no longer romantic partners. Not that it would matter if we were."

Sara relaxed into her chair and watched the tiny ripples in her dark tea. The polyamorous nature of the Cortese family wasn't unusual for Amoran people. The Amora Goddesses paired people through the magic in their souls. Stephen was Sara's first soulmate, but he wasn't her only and unlikely her last.

"Thank you," Sara said quietly. Her gaze shifted slightly from her teacup to Stephen, who grinned at her in the most irritating of ways.

She put down her cup and decided to change the subject to one simmering in the back of her mind.

"Did the bards perform? Some villagers have said their news has been most concerning. Their tales are already so dramatized, and I'm unsure if what I'm hearing secondhand is true."

Stephen sighed and ran his hand down his long beard a few times until the end came to a neat curl. "Yes. Their news was a bit worrisome. You may want to get your journal for this."

Sara frowned and reached for the book beside her.

"There's always been those who distance themselves from Amoran culture and make a life better suited for themselves," Stephen began. "But this is different. The intention is different."

"What's their intention?" Sara asked, unease growing in her belly.

"To dismantle Amoran communities by sowing distrust of the Goddesses."

Stone-like stillness replaced the ease in Stephen's posture.

"A faction that calls itself the Commarasi travels the continent, settling in struggling villages. The Commarasi convince the villagers to lay the blame for their suffering at the feet of the Goddesses and their earthly councils."

Stephen paused to drink his tea, allowing Sara to make some notes.

"The bards spoke of villages in the mountains and plains of Arcanos where the elders have died without naming successors and the remaining villagers fight amongst themselves for power. Commarasi leaders put restrictions on magic so that it benefits few instead of all. There is no more shared abundance."

Sara was afraid to give voice to the most frightening news she'd heard, but she drummed up the courage to ask. "And the women? I heard they—"

"Are stripped of their independence," Stephen finished for her. His demeanor shifted with restrained anger.

"But why?" Sara asked, though she already knew the answer.

Amoran children inherit their magic from the soul of the body that created them. Feminine and birthing people are no more powerful than the masculine people of their village, but it's their magic that flows within the family line.

"The Commarasi are so detached from their ancestral traditions that they've become willfully ignorant and spread false beliefs," said Stephen, his knuckles turning white as he gripped his cup. "Women can't lead businesses or own property on their own. They must have at least one masculine partner to share it with. And they no longer hold any political or spiritual titles."

Sara slouched in her seat, disappointed that Stephen's version matched what she had heard from others.

"What about the children and their training?" she asked after sitting in contemplative silence for some time. Amora are born with magic, but it must be developed like any other skill. Their magic will lie dormant without that training and eventually weaken until it can no longer be accessed.

Stephen confirmed what Sara already suspected. "Parents forgo the teaching of magic, either by force or by choice, and their sacred rituals are forgotten. Without magic, or the free use of whatever remains, villages become susceptible to malevolent creatures from Teremedi. It doesn't take long for the village to fall and a generation of Amora to vanish."

Sara blew out a harsh breath.

"Our children will be fine," Stephen said, reaching over and taking Sara's hand. "Belhaven is an island, and that will offer us protection that other villages don't have. Our ties to the Goddesses are strong. Our rituals and festivals are lively and faith remains."

Sara managed a weak smile. Sara was prone to pessimism, and Stephen's rational pragmatism often set her mind at ease. He'd always been an empathetic counterbalance. But something in Belhaven felt different this time, and a stone of dread sat heavy in her stomach.

CHAPTER 6

BETHANY

Bethany slammed the door to John Dawson's bedroom and stood with her back against the cool wood. Her body tensed at the sound of glass shattering against the door. She slid down to the floor, pulled her knees to her chest, and listened to her charge weeping softly.

In her quarter of a century as a healing doula, Bethany had never experienced anything like John's illness. Between the pain and lack of sleep, John was unpleasant on his best days and downright mean on his worst. She convinced his wife Rebekah to take their youngest children to their uncles' home on the other side of the island. It would spare them the memories of their father screaming obscenities at their mother.

Piper bounded into the house through the door closest to her workshop. "Are you okay? Did he hurt you?"

She still wore her smithing apron and heavy gloves. Dark ash streaked across her forehead from where she must have wiped her brow.

"I'm fine," Bethany sighed. "Your father isn't the first patient to throw something at me."

"That doesn't make me feel any better," Piper said as she pulled Bethany up from the ground.

Bethany was mindlessly rubbing her aching shoulder when she heard Sara's hurried footsteps entering the house. Bethany felt Sara's pulsing magic the moment the other woman crossed the threshold. It seemed to beat in time with Bethany's own heart. Curiously, Piper stood inches away, and hers barely feathered over Bethany's skin.

She didn't have a chance to contemplate it before Sara rushed over.

"What happened?" Sara wore a look of concern but kept an even composure.

"My father happened." Piper took off her gloves and rubbed her face. "I'm so sorry, Bethany."

Bethany smiled and put a hand on Piper's shoulder. "You don't need to apologize, Piper. Your father is feeling terrible, and he's not sleeping. Lashing out is expected."

Piper sighed. "It's still not okay."

Sara pulled the young woman into an embrace and whispered reassurance in Piper's ear. Bethany wanted to comfort Piper also, but she was distracted and flustered by Sara's unexpected presence.

"What brings you here, Sara?" Bethany finally asked. "Did we make plans to meet? Did I forget?"

Sara had been by the previous day with new tonics and ointments to replace the ones that no longer provided John any relief. Bethany didn't expect her at the Dawson home for another couple of days.

"No, no. I just . . ." Sara trailed off and tucked a strand of her chestnut hair behind her ear. "You looked so frazzled yesterday that I thought you could use a break and might like to join me for a midday meal."

Bethany hadn't known her for very long, but she had yet to encounter this shy and unsure version of Sara. When she spoke of her work and her love of plants, it was always with confidence and excitement.

Bethany would happily spend an eternity sharing meals with Sara, but she didn't want to take Piper away from her work to mind her father.

"I shouldn't," Bethany choked.

"But you will," Piper insisted. "Leave my home and don't come back until you've had some time to eat and rest."

"But what about your work?" Bethany said, trying and failing to fight against Piper herding the older women toward the door. Working with heavy tools gave Piper muscular arms and legs that she was using to physically force Bethany into taking some time for herself.

"My father won't have any chance of coming back to work if your light burns out, Bethany!" Piper—lovingly—shoved Bethany and Sara into the garden and locked the door behind them.

Sara shook with laughter, tears beginning to well in the corners of her hazel eyes. Her sun-bronzed light skin was red as a cardinal. The delightful sound was a balm to Bethany's tired soul, and she couldn't fight it even if she wanted to.

"Well then," Bethany said with a laugh. "I guess I'm yours for the afternoon."

"I guess you are." Sara's sparkling eyes darkened. She bit her plump lower lip, but it couldn't hide her devilish grin. "Follow me."

Sara led her into the forest beyond the Dawson's garden. They followed a lightly worn path winding between towering pines and thick oaks. Bethany's eyes darted between the trail and the lush vegetation around her. A million shades of green against dark and light browns, and the occasional pop of red, yellow, or purple. Bethany didn't spend much time amongst the trees. Not like Sara who walked the trail with the surety of someone in a familiar place. Magic connected the earth to Sara and Sara to the earth.

The sound of rushing water joined the forest's song, and a wide creek came into view. The water slowed and bubbled as it flowed over boulders worn smooth over millennia. Tadpoles and finger-long fish swam in circles in shallow pools along the bank.

Bethany dipped her fingers into the cold water, and magic from the earth joined the gentle current. Even with nature's beauty around her, Bethany could only observe Sara. She pulled a blanket from her satchel and shook it out until it lay flat in the dappled sunlight of a towering magnolia. She set out a loaf of bread, sheep's cheese, and several small jars of jams and sour pickles.

Leaving the peacefulness of the creek, Bethany joined Sara on the blanket.

"Are these from Anna Hartley's farm?" Bethany asked. She tore a chunk off the loaf and opened one of the unlabeled jars of dark pink jam.

"They are. Have you met her family yet?" Sara answered between bites.

"She dropped off a basket the day I arrived, but our introduction got cut short when her littlest one toddled into some horse droppings."

Sara nearly gagged on the pickle she was chewing and laughed between raspy coughs. It delighted Bethany how easily Sara laughed, which was fortunate since Bethany didn't consider herself very funny.

"Poor woman has her hands full, that's for sure," Sara said finally. "Carson, her oldest, is still learning how to control their magic. They used a bit too much on the plums last season, so the village spent the entire winter eating their weight in plum jam."

These sorts of miscalculations were common among young, verdant magi. Their earth magic complements their farming skills passed down through generations. The bountiful crop is shared with the community so no one goes hungry, even in lean winters.

Bethany smiled at the layer of jam on her bread. "There are worse things to have an overabundance of."

She took another bite, letting the taste of summers past roll over her tongue.

"I'm ashamed to admit I've been forgetting to eat lately," she confessed. "John requires so much care and even if I notice my body telling me it needs nourishment, I'm often too exhausted to eat. This is the first meal I've had sitting down in weeks."

Bethany felt immense guilt anytime she took time for herself, and her inability to put her needs first was a constant argument between her and her former partner, Fredrick. Before she and Fredrick parted ways, she made a promise to him and their daughter Adessa she would change, but it was a promise she often failed to keep.

Until Sara.

"Well," Sara said firmly, her lips curling into a smile. "Then I will personally see to it that you eat, even if I must feed you myself!"

Sara grabbed whatever she could reach and piled it on Bethany's plate. The more Bethany laughed, the taller the precarious tower of fruit and cheese and bread became.

"Enough! Stop!" Her stomach hurt and her eyes watered.

Sara sat back on her heels, a look of great satisfaction on her face. The green in her hazel eyes matched the drooping ferns nearby. The delicate wrinkles and strands of white typical for her age couldn't outshine Sara's mirth.

Bethany regained her composure but nearly lost it again when Sara shook her finger and said, "Don't test me, Bethany. All three of my babies were stubborn eaters. I know all the tricks."

Bethany tore off a hunk of bread with her teeth. Looking satisfied, Sara relaxed on the blanket.

"I wish I had more tricks for John," Sara said thoughtfully. "His illness is quite the mystery."

Bethany sighed heavily. For her, it was more than just a mystery, it felt wrong and a violation of the life cycle Amora hold dear.

"I think it's an omen of terrible times ahead," Bethany admitted aloud for the first time. "I worry that whatever illness plagues him will begin the loss of faith in our Goddesses."

Sara sucked in a breath and twisted her loose hair in her small hands. But her eyes remained on Bethany, urging her on.

The dam was open, and she wanted to spill her worries to this woman who was still mostly a stranger but felt like a piece of her. So she continued.

"I heard rumors that some of the elders believe that a nefarious spirit walks among us."

Sara's gaze shifted to the ground. "What do you think? You're more attuned to magic than others."

Bethany considered Sara's question and how evasive she'd suddenly become.

"Something feels wrong," Bethany said finally.

Sara turned towards the creek, and Bethany followed her gaze to a family of white deer that stopped for a drink.

"You know it's against my duties to the council to repeat what is said during their private meetings," Sara said, her eyes still on the sensitive animals. "But my oath is to the people of our village. So I will tell you this: What you suspect has been discussed."

Bethany nodded, understanding the trust that Sara had just put in her.

Sara eased back on her hands, her back arching slightly and lifting her breasts a bit higher for a breath of a moment. Feeling the heat spread across her face, Bethany turned her head back to the water.

They sat quietly for some time. The intimate silence soothed Bethany's nerves after sharing such vulnerable thoughts. Water tumbled over the rocks, joining the harmony of birdsong and the breeze rustling through the trees.

Bethany took a sip of ale, and Sara broke the silence. "Why do you keep making that face?"

"What face?" Bethany questioned.

"Every time you move your right arm a certain way, you make a face," Sara insisted, sitting up straight.

"I do no such thing!" Bethany gasped. But in truth, she'd been dealing with the aches in her shoulder for so long she hardly noticed.

"Liar! You look like this." Sara twisted her features into an exaggerated cringe that surely Bethany would have noticed if it happened as often as Sara claimed.

Bethany covered her mouth to hide her laughter, but the more she tried to hide it, the more ridiculous Sara looked. When she couldn't contain herself anymore, she allowed the laughter to break free, making her belly ache and her eyes water once again.

"Fine!" Bethany cried. "You are insufferable!"

Sara smiled a broad grin with her charmingly crooked teeth.

"I don't even notice the aches anymore," Bethany said as she visually scanned her joints. "I've been caring for our people for almost thirty years, and it's taken a toll on my body. My patients often need help moving, and sometimes I'm the only one to aid them in this way."

Bethany didn't think it was much different from other villagers who use their body in their work. Piper Dawson was only in her early twenties and already complained of pains in her wrists and elbows. At some point, Piper would seek treatment, whereas Bethany would always put the needs of her patients first.

Sara nodded, a thoughtful look on her face. "Hand me my satchel, would you?"

While Bethany reached for the satchel, Sara scooted back until she could lean against the wide magnolia.

"Come. I have a balm that will help." Sara dug through the cavernous bag until she found a small jar.

Bethany hesitated, overwhelmed by the care that Sara continued to offer. Sara opened her legs and patted the ground between her knees in an insistent but gentle invitation. Bethany's eyes blurred as she slid closer to settle herself between Sara's thighs.

"I've always been treated well by our people, but few have ever offered to care for me in the way you do," Bethany said, feeling emboldened by the lack of eye contact.

"You're worthy of care," Sara said simply. "And I understand it can be hard to put yourself first."

Bethany sat with Sara's words while she undid the lacing of her bodice and the neckline of her tunic. The flowing fabric slid to one side, exposing her shoulder and bicep.

The thick balm melted in the warmth of Sara's hands against Bethany's skin. The fragrant scent of maypops danced in the air around them. She could almost taste their sweet fruit exploding on her tongue. Bethany moaned softly as Sara pressed her fingers into the tender spots.

The mixture worked quickly to ease Bethany's shoulder pain, then spread through her body to find her other aches. Sara's magic swirled with Bethany's in a way that didn't just heal her muscles and swollen joints; it connected their souls.

Sara

Working in silence, Sara massaged the balm into Bethany's muscles until the tension eased under her fingertips. She observed every dark freckle on Bethany's light skin, committing the location of each one to memory.

She traveled down Bethany's arm, taking special care of the soft space inside of her wrist. Sara lingered there, mesmerized by the rhythm of Bethany's heart beating under the delicate skin.

Her thumb slid over Bethany's palm with steady, even pressure. A whimpered sigh slipped from Bethany's lips. Sara registered a subtle shift in the energy surrounding them, though she didn't know what it meant.

"There is so much anger and sadness in John's body," Bethany said, her voice as loose as her posture. "Just being in his presence is draining. Every day he worsens, and every day I have to work harder to ease his suffering."

They'd never spoken this candidly before, and in an odd way, it comforted Sara to know someone else felt it too.

"I leave his home with such heavy sadness," Sara confided.

Again she found herself curling her fingers with Bethany's, but this time not just to provide comfort but to receive it. "I thought it was because I was watching my friend suffer, but it's more than that. It feels like it's coming from inside him."

Bethany turned around until their eyes locked. Sara mapped every shade of green in Bethany's emerald eyes. The exhaustion in her face remained, but there was something else there.

Yearning? Hunger?

Sara wanted it to be so. She would gladly let Bethany feast upon her if it would tip the scales towards happiness.

The magic around them shifted again, stronger this time, a magnetic pull that was impossible to ignore. Bethany's fingertips danced over Sara's face until her hand settled on Sara's cheek. The lightness of her touch was at odds with the strength of whatever brought them closer.

Sara relaxed into Bethany's palm. Their foreheads touched.

"It's only when you're by my side that I remember what happiness feels like," Bethany whispered. Her breath brushed over Sara's mouth and severed the tether holding her back.

Sara pushed forward, pressing their lips together with a contented sigh. Bethany's lips were sticky with the summer sweetness of plum jam and soothed an ache Sara didn't know she had. She'd wanted this from the moment they'd met, but Sara wasn't expecting it to feel like finding a missing piece of her soul.

Pulling away slightly, Sara said, "I wasn't done, you know."

"Oh? But you've already done so much."

Sara sat up and wordlessly guided Bethany's lush hips to settle again between her legs.

"Let me care for you, Bethy." Sara traced a finger down the curve of her neck to Bethany's still exposed shoulder. Her dull nails left a pink line that she followed with featherlight kisses.

Bethany's breath quickened, her pulse pounding against Sara's lips. She tipped her head back, exposing more of her long neck for Sara to kiss.

"Let me care for your body," Sara whispered.

Slipping her hands under the loose fabric, Sara's fingers roamed Bethany's dimpled belly. A river of scars flowed up and down Bethany's torso, like a map that would lead to her pleasure. Following them up, Sara found the pillowy softness of Bethany's heavy breasts. They rose and fell with the quickening pace of her breath.

One hand remained on Bethany's breast, her thumb making small circles around her stiff nipple. The other scooped a dollop of ointment from the jar discarded nearby.

"Let me ease your aches," she whispered against the flush of Bethany's neck.

The pads of her fingers slid over Bethany's chest, finding the tender muscles beneath. Sara lavished attention on each one, drinking in every cry and whimper that spilled from Bethany's lips.

She was determined to make Bethany see that she was worthy of care. That she deserved rest and to be fed. She deserved comfort and pleasure. Sara firmly believed the Goddesses brought them together for this reason.

Sara once again followed the river down hills and valleys of Bethany's waist, stopping at the band of her trousers.

Bethany arched her back with a gasp of anticipation followed by a whine of disappointment.

"Let me fill your body with pleasure."

"Yes," Bethany pleaded, digging her fingers into Sara's thigh.

"Yes, what?" Sara teased her, wiggling her fingers just under the waistband.

"Please fill my body with pleasure," Bethany breathed.

"Good girl," Sara whispered and popped the button on Bethany's trousers, allowing her hands more movement.

Bethany's body softened with an exhale, then stiffened when Sara ran two fingers between her legs, collecting Bethany's wet desire on her fingertips.

Sara lavished attention on Bethany's pussy the same way she did her breasts. She catalogued every subtle response to every change in touch.

Like the way Bethany melted when Sara's fingers slid inside her folds.

Or the way she moaned when Sara rubbed her clit hard and quick. She wanted to know what made Bethany dig her nails into Sara's legs.

What kind of touch caused her hips to thrust.

What made her whimper and what made her writhe.

She wanted to know what Bethany's cries of ecstasy sounded like.

"Let go, Bethy," Sara cooed.

Bethany released everything with a primal cry that echoed through the forest.

When her gasping breaths slowed to sated sighs, Sara gently returned Bethany to her formerly dressed state. She leaned back against the tree, settling Bethany's limp body against her heated chest. Bethany's eyelids fluttered heavily.

”Sleep, love,” Sara whispered in her ear.
Bethany sighed a laugh and let go.

Chapter 7

Bethany

It was too early in the morning for a battle of wills with
a seagull, but Bethany refused to let the stubborn bird
steal her breakfast. She rarely had such a quiet morning.
John's wife Rebekah returned home for the day to care for
her husband while Bethany and Sara journeyed to Willow
Ridge.

The Amora temple in Willow Ridge was the largest in
Valen's southern region and housed a robust library where
Sara hoped to find more spells to aid in John's treatment.
While Sara combed the stacks, Bethany would seek counsel
from her elder healers. With more than 100 years of
knowledge between them, surely they would be able to
provide some guidance.

That's what she was counting on anyway.

Sara's magic danced over Bethany's skin like saltwater
mist caught in the breeze. Bethany turned away from the
water, and the sight made her momentarily breathless. Sara
looked radiant in a creamy linen dress that flowed softly
behind her. It had no sleeves, but she covered her shoulders
and arms from the sun with a light shawl embroidered with
orange and red flowers. The dark purple bodice cinched
at the waist highlighted her soft, round hips. Her hair was
pinned away from her face with gemstone combs and
twisted into a long braid.

Distracted by the approaching woman, Bethany let her guard down long enough for the gull to steal her last biscuit.

"Hey!" Bethany yelled at the bird.

Sara's boisterous laugh cut through Bethany's irritation with the sneaky animal.

"This is your fault," Bethany said to Sara.

Sara arched a brow. "How do you figure?"

"You distracted me."

"So don't be so distractable," Sara said with a coy smile.

Bethany leaned in, her lips fluttering over Sara's. "Don't be so distracting."

They shared a chaste kiss that felt anything but.

If not for the ferry docking nearby, Bethany would have considered calling off the entire trip and having her way with the other woman.

"We'll finish this later," Bethany said, her turn to be coy.

They walked up to the ferry hand-in-hand and waited patiently as half a dozen people stepped off the craft carrying various wares they were trying to sell or trade.

The strip of sea between Belhaven's southern coast and the continental mainland was known for its calm waters and easy passage to and from Willow Ridge. Trade was common and necessary between the two villages.

The same couldn't be said for the sea on Belhaven's north side, where the coast of Valen sat farther than Willow Ridge and was partially exposed to the open ocean. The waters were often rough, and inexperienced passage was unwise during most times of the year.

"Climb aboard, ladies," the ferryman called with a wave of his cap. His dark brown skin glistened with sweat, and he wiped his brow before replacing the head covering.

"Good morning, Joseph!" They called. He was the same ferryman that transported Bethany to her new life in Belhaven.

Bethany wobbled on the gangplank, and Sara placed a supportive hand on her back. The intoxicating warmth of Sara's magic flowed through Bethany's body like blood through her veins.

The women settled themselves near the bow and exchanged pleasantries with Joseph while they waited for any additional passengers. When it was clear no one else would be making the journey, the sails of the vessel caught the gentle breeze, and it lurched forward with a groan.

"The trip will be a bit longer than usual, I'm afraid," Joseph shouted from the wheel once they were on the way. "Without a sea goat aiding us, I'll only have whatever power the winds will give me."

When he transported Bethany to Belhaven, Joseph had the wind in his sails and the assistance of the dolphin-sized sea creature guiding the craft forward.

"What happened to it?" Bethany asked.

"I set it free," he said with a hint of sadness. The animal was never imprisoned, but the Amora animal keepers that work the waters often have strong bonds with the creatures that work beside them.

"Something is causing all the animals great distress," Joseph continued. "They're generally pretty docile, and they've become unusually aggressive. I saw one tear apart a seal a few days ago."

Sara's eyes widened with a loud gasp, and Bethany gave the other woman's leg a comforting squeeze.

"When my most reliable goat nearly capsized one of my larger ships, I knew it was time. I said goodbye, and I haven't seen it—or any others—since. I suspect it returned to Teremedi with the rest of them."

Bethany watched Sara's face turn curious, like she was working a puzzle in her mind. Her eyes narrowed, and her nose scrunched just slightly.

"The animal keepers in Belhaven speak of the same," Sara finally said. "They think it's connected to the Commarasi."

"How so?" Bethany asked.

They didn't talk much about the Commarasi and the group's attempts to rid the Arcanos continent of Amoran culture. When working, the women focused only on topics related to John's treatment and care. And in their rare moments alone, Sara filled Bethany's body with the kind of euphoria that ignited her soul.

But while Bethany seldom spent time where this kind of information spread quickly, Sara's title as keeper of lore required her to keep public records of news circulating through the village.

Bethany never saw Sara without a journal and writing instrument nearby. Sara could be forgetful with the most mundane things, but Bethany marveled at Sara's ability to remember her conversations with others. Perhaps that was the trade when the Goddesses chose this fate for her.

"The gatekeepers that guard the rifts between the realms are being pulled from their posts to fight the Commarasi where their uprisings have become violent," Sara explained. "More malevolent creatures have been able to pass through."

Joseph nodded. "That's a rational explanation. I'm not sure what we can do about it, however."

Bethany felt Sara's energy shift only moments before her face changed from curiosity to concern, her knee bouncing under Bethany's hand. Bethany squeezed it gently until it settled. Their eyes met, and Bethany offered her a reassuring smile.

"The gatekeepers are our most skilled fighters," replied Bethany. She was speaking to both but looked only at Sara. "I'm sure they can quell the violence and return to their posts before anything truly evil passes through."

The rest of their voyage was filled with less serious discussions, and the time passed quickly. They docked in Willow Ridge and made arrangements with Joseph for their journey back to Belhaven.

Bethany took Sara's hand and guided her through the bustling port village. Belhaven had its own lively energy, but it differed in a way that Bethany was growing to prefer. The people of Willow Ridge rushed through the market district like they had important places to be and a long list of things to do. They were kind and polite but didn't linger in conversation with friends or acquaintances.

Belhaven had a vibrant energy, but it didn't come from village folk rushing from place to place. It came from the excitement of catching up with a friend or showing off a new piece of art. It came from the drama that always spawned when people knew each other too well. She'd lived in many places during her forty rotations around the sun, and Willow Ridge was always her home base.

But Belhaven was quickly becoming her home.

There was so much in her hometown that Bethany wanted Sara to experience, but it would all have to wait until they finished with their research and likely require another trip.

In the center of the chaos stood the grand Amora temple and its library. Before heading inside, Bethany gave Sara some time to stare at the opulent structure. Bethany drank in Sara's look of wonder marked by the way her hazel eyes widened, letting the light illuminate the deep brown until it looked like amber.

"Go play," Bethany said, urging Sara toward the door. "I'll find you when I'm finished with the elders."

Sara kissed Bethany's cheek and sprinted for the door, her boots kicking up dirt behind her.

CHAPTER 8

SARA

The library towered over the coastline, and from its large windows, Sara gazed at her island home in the middle of a blue sea. At this height, she could make out Belhaven's village center hidden amongst giant pines. Watching the roll of the tide soothed the frustration that came from poring over book after book with little success.

She was looking for anything that could do more than just slow John Dawson's worsening symptoms. She found little more than what she'd already tried and was no closer to determining the actual cause.

When she finally had enough, she changed course, looking for anything that could strengthen Bethany or help her recover more quickly. Bethany tried to deny her fatigue, but her body displayed the toll of her work for all to see. The texture of her golden-brown hair turned brittle and started losing its curl. Her light skin had taken on a gray hue.

Bethany was always burning her candle too low and expending more of her vital energy than she'd replenish. Sara's magic was meant to support her during times like this, but every day John worsened, and Sara's spells became less effective.

With the looming fear of Bethany healing herself to death, Sara sifted through a dozen books, pulling anything and everything that held any potential. She sought a respite at the nearest window when her eyes began to blur. She was tracking the flight of a seagull when the warm embrace of Bethany's magic twisted with hers. Sara welcomed it and the tingling sensation it brought to her body.

Unlike John, the twining of their magic strengthened every day.

Between the sweet vibrations and the hypnotic movement of the water below, a calmness washed over Sara that she hadn't felt in some time. The worry that plagued her was taken and returned to the sea.

Bethany's hands slid around Sara's waist until their bodies pressed together tightly. There wasn't much of a height difference between the two women, but Bethany was tall enough that she could rest her chin on Sara's shoulder. Bethany kissed the crook of Sara's neck, and she leaned into it with a quiet giggle.

"I knew you'd be here before I even stepped in the building," Bethany said, nuzzling deeper.

Sara leaned into Bethany's warmth, pressing her cheek against the other woman's and interlocking their fingers. "And why is that?"

"Because it's perfectly you."

Sara chuckled and felt Bethany's cheeks lift into a smile. "That's not a proper answer."

"Well." Bethany accented the word with another kiss to Sara's neck. "It's on the same level as all the books you'd likely reference. These large windows let in the most light because they have a clear view of the sea. And like the plants that you often seek, you thrive in the light and wither in darkness."

"I don't wither," Sara balked. "That's a bit harsh."

"Hush." Bethany playfully grazed her teeth against Sara's neck and squeezed her tighter. "The windows closer to the stacks where you pulled your books from also have a clear view of the sea. A better view, many would say. But from this window, you can see the coastal forest below. Because for as much as you adore the sea, you are a child of the forest and prefer dirt under your feet."

Sara grinned at the accurate description. She did first consider the tables near the windows closest to the alchemist texts, but for reasons she couldn't articulate, she chose this spot because it felt right.

Sara wasn't ready to move or break from their embrace, but she wanted to know if Bethany had better luck. "How did your talk with the elders go?"

Bethany forced out a frustrated breath and slumped a bit into Sara's back. "Not as well as I had hoped. The elders have never seen anything like this, but they've heard of others contracting an illness with similar symptoms. There's no evidence that they're connected, though. Until there is, they said to keep quiet about it because the Commarasi are causing enough anxiety. So don't go writing about it just y et."

Sara scoffed, but she knew Bethany was only teasing. "I don't write down everything, Bethy. It would take me hours to pen these entries if I did."

"I'd like to read them one day," Bethany said, the lightness returning to her voice. "I want to know what kind of things our descendants will learn about me. I'm sure it's just the filthy things, like those erotic books you and Piper share."

A laugh erupted from Sara with such force it echoed across the large space. She slapped her hands over her mouth to stifle the sound, but it only made her laugh harder. So much of their time spent together was solemn and serious, and it was during these times that Bethany made Sara laugh the hardest.

"Sara, don't be so loud in the library," Bethany taunted. "You need to keep your voice down."

Bethany egged her on until Sara's stomach hurt and tears streamed down her face. "Bethy, please stop," Sara gasped through her giggles. "I don't wish to spend the rest of this journey in soiled undergarments."

Bethany sighed and kissed Sara's neck again. "Okay."

Bethany slowed her breathing, coaxing Sara to do the same until their chests rose and fell together as they watched the serene roll of the tide below.

"Did your midwife not arrange for you to be seen by a healing doula after your babies were born?" Bethany asked.

Sara smiled at the slight professional annoyance in her tone.

"I did after Eleanor and Lenni, but Louis was born during a baby boom on the island, and he was the most challenging infant of all." Sara barely remembered those early years. With so many children coming into the world, the whole village was stretched thin as everyone aided exhausted parents.

"I had less complications than other birth givers, and the strengthening movements the midwife taught me were very helpful," Sara recalled. "The gentle stomach contractions were easy enough to do throughout the day. But I just kept forgetting to meet with our healer. And I don't regret it—or think about it—until someone makes me laugh or I sneeze too hard and it soaks my undergarments."

Bethany laughed through her nose. "Well, few birthing injuries are too far gone to be healed, should you want to laugh or sneeze without worry."

"Ahh what a joyous life that would be," Sara teased.

After a beat, Sara said, "We don't talk much about babies, you and me. I never ask because so many of us have experienced heartbreak and pain."

Bethany's body stiffened but loosened again with a sigh.

"I have experienced heartbreak," Bethany said.

"Oh," Sara whispered sadly and tightened her grip on Bethany's embrace.

"But not in the way you're thinking." Bethany's tone lightened. She pressed her forehead against Sara's temple. "It's a long story for another day. Tell me about your research."

Their bodies parted, and as they returned to the piles of books scattered around the table, Sara told Bethany about what little she'd found. Their excursion to Willow Ridge didn't yield the information they were looking for, but she felt rejuvenated by her time in a new place and in the quiet of the library.

When they were finished putting the texts back in their rightful places, Sara took another long look around the space.

"So do you have a spot in this library that's perfectly you?" she asked Bethany.

Bethany's head tilted to the side while she considered Sara's question. "I didn't spend as much time here as other magic users, but yes, I do have a spot."

Sara didn't miss the darkening of Bethany's emerald eyes and the way the corners of her mouth lifted into a devilish smile. It sent heat through her body, and her heartbeat raced.

Bethany beckoned her with a finger, spun around, and headed toward the opposite end of the floor. Sara usually kept up with Bethany's naturally quick strides, but she almost lost her at this hastened pace. She followed Bethany around the library's twisting stacks and up the stone steps to the top of the tallest spire.

With fewer windows came less light, and it took Sara's eyes some time to adjust to the darkness. Bethany slowed, giving Sara the opportunity to observe the collection as they caught their breath. Around her were ledgers and journals holding official records written by scribes like herself. Amongst the books were dusty artifacts from unknown times and places. Sara wanted to stop and explore it all, but Bethany's magic lured her forward. She caught up to her lover in a nook lit by the small windows above their heads. Around them were nearly empty bookshelves and a few dusty tables.

Bethany was a temptress that Sara couldn't resist. She was grateful to the Goddesses that Bethany had no ill intent because the enchanting woman could ruin Sara's life, and she would thank her for the opportunity.

Sara closed the gap between them and threaded her fingers into her lover's hair, guiding Bethany's mouth to hers. Their lips danced together lightly with delicious restraint.

"How many paramours have you brought here?" Sara murmured, aroused by the thought of Bethany experiencing clandestine pleasure.

"Many."

"Tell me about them."

Bethany's teeth grazed over Sara's bottom lip, and she opened her mouth wider for a sweep of Bethany's tongue.

Bethany took Sara's waist in her hungry grip. The back of Sara's legs found the edge of the table, halting the playful roughness that had them swaying around the small space.

"I hated book studies," Bethany said as she untied the lacing of Sara's bodice. With every loosening pull, Sara let out a small whimper of feverish anticipation.

"I'd get so bored."

Once the bodice fell loose, Bethany started untying the lace on the bust of Sara's dress.

"And what did you do when you were bored?" Sara panted, breathless from the carnal ache between her thighs.

Bethany didn't answer. She dragged her teeth over bottom lip, dark and swollen from their frenzied kisses.

"I'd go for a walk," Bethany said with the last pull of lace. The cool air hit Sara's exposed breasts. Her knees buckled when Bethany's lips met her peaked nipple.

Sara placed one hand on the table to keep herself upright, while using the other to run her fingertips over Bethany's scalp. Overwhelmed by the pleasure of Bethany's soft lips and the circling of her tongue, she gripped Bethany's hair with a gentle, but needy tug.

Pulling away from Sara, Bethany stood up straight. She whined from the sudden absence, and Bethany replied with a teasing grin.

"Occasionally on these walks," Bethany continued, "I'd find a friend from the village who was also bored with their studies."

She picked up the skirt of Sara's dress and instructed her to sit on the table. Sara complied and watched silently as Bethany bunched up the fabric, tucking it between her body and the table to offer a bit of padding.

"Are you comfortable?" Bethany asked.

Sara nodded, but she would have dealt with any amount of discomfort for the sweet relief of orgasmic bliss.

Bethany ran a finger over the hem of Sara's undergarments, knowingly building Sara's needy desire. "And we'd come to this spot because, as you can see, few people ever have a need to be up here."

"How convenient," Sara breathed, overcome with vivid fantasies of Bethany finding her and pulling her from her studies. Academics had been a struggle for Sara. Bethany could have been her greatest motivation or biggest distraction.

Bethany pulled down Sara's undergarments until they fell to her boots, leaving her raw and exposed and desperate to be touched and toyed with.

"Yes," Bethany breathed. Her hands slid up the inside of Sara's thighs, coaxing them open even wider. Despite how tired Bethany's body appeared, her eyes were awake with fire and lust.

"But remember, Sara, this is a library. So even up here, you must be quiet."

Even if she had the right words, Sara didn't have a chance to respond; Bethany's tongue landed on Sara's clit, and she threw her head back with a gasp.

Devouring Sara's tender flesh, she dug her fingers into Sara's plush hips, her hands grazing over the long marks left from carrying new life. Enough light leaked through the windows to illuminate Bethany's cheeks flushed with scarlet heat, and chin wet with Sara's lust.

Sara struggled to temper the sounds of erotic oblivion, and with every too-loud moan, Bethany would smile against her cunt, and tongue fuck Sara even harder.

Bethany pulled back, and Sara grieved the loss of Bethany's mouth with a whimpered pout.

"Shhhh, Sara," Bethany hushed.

But a cry escaped Sara's lips when Bethany slid a finger inside her.

"We're in a library, love. You must keep quiet while I fuck you."

The sound that Sara made next was something like a laugh, then a sigh, and finally a restrained gasp when Bethany added a second finger. Sara rolled her hips in blissful rhythm with Bethany. Sara's arms burned from keeping her upright, but she was hypnotized by the way Bethany responded to her body, giving Sara everything she needed before she knew she wanted it.

Their magic swirled together and pulsed with energy created by their passion. It flowed through Sara's veins, bringing pleasure to all the deep corners of her body. Greedy for more, she thrust her hips to take Bethany's fingers harder and deeper.

Euphoria arrived, and Sara welcomed it with a silent, breathless cry. She didn't dare allow even a sigh for fear that her moans would echo across the solemn space. Her arms gave out, and she collapsed onto her back. Bethany massaged Sara's clit, extending the ripples of the pleasure she'd brought to Sara's body until she came again.

Bethany gingerly pulled up Sara's undergarments, leaving a trail of kisses between her thighs. Sara sat up, and Bethany helped her off the table, supporting her when she wobbled on weak legs.

Sara pawed at Bethany's clothing, desperate to bury her face between the other woman's thighs.

Bethany laughed and stopped her.

"But I want to," Sara began.

Bethany silenced her with a chaste kiss. "I know. But if you do, I fear we'll miss our ferry back to Belhaven."

Sara rolled her eyes, but Bethany was probably right. She released a frustrated sigh and finished getting dressed.

"You never answered my question," Sara said as she rebraided her hair.

Bethany narrowed her eyes in confusion.

"Many is not a number, silly." Sara smiled.

Bethany laughed. "Two."

"Two isn't many!" Sara argued.

"No, it's not. And one was my former husband when we were about Piper's age. But you love an erotic story, so I told you one."

"Well," Sara huffed and crossed her arms. "It was very good. Maybe you could come up with a few more details, and I could write it down."

"So we can fill up the family library with tales of lust?" Bethany smiled wickedly.

Sara took hold of Bethany's chin, still gloriously sticky and tempting Sara enough to consider missing their ferry.

"Not the whole library. Just a few volumes." Sara planted a light kiss on Bethany's swollen lips. "The rest would be tales of love."

CHAPTER 9

SARA

The late day sun was already hidden behind Belhaven's tallest conifer trees when Sara and Bethany set foot back on Belhaven. Sara yawned, and her stomach growled.

"I'm hungry too," Bethany said with a bright smile.

Bethany had fallen asleep while they waited for Joseph to arrive and dozed off again shortly after they boarded the craft. Sara, on the other hand, had no trouble staying awake, but now that they were close to home, she longed for some warm bread with butter and a nap.

"Sara!" A familiar voice called.

Both women turned toward the sound. A young man about Piper Dawson's age jogged up to them. It was Charles, the assistant to the Council of Nine.

"Is everything okay?" she asked, her panic rising. "My children . . ."

"Yes. I'm sorry for the scare," he panted, waving his hands for emphasis. "Your children are fine. As far as I know of course."

Sara stared at him with her hands on her hips as he took a few deep breaths.

"The elders want to see you and Bethany immediately," he said, fixing the lopsided cap covering his short blond hair.

"Can't it wait?" Bethany grumbled. "I need to see to John Dawson. We were in Willow Ridge all day."

"That's why they wish to see you," he said, finally catching his breath and wiping his brow with the sleeve of his tunic.

Sara groaned. "Fine. But we haven't eaten yet. Please have something prepared for when we arrive."

"Good idea," Bethany whispered.

Charles acknowledged her request with a "yes, ma'am," and a curt nod before jogging back toward the temple. Sara and Bethany followed but refused to meet his speedy pace.

"Are the elders usually so insistent?" Bethany asked.

"Not unless it's urgent," Sara replied. "But their definition of what constitutes as urgent is constantly evolving, and more discussions have been considered *urgent* as of late."

Sara couldn't remember a time when her mentor was called to so many meetings on such short notice. The village and the surrounding region were experiencing new challenges, but few required the haste the elders demanded. Most of their meetings could have been a bulletin posted in the village square.

The temple was quiet, save for a few villagers leaving offerings on the altars for the Goddesses and in the communal spaces where Amora shared their abundance with neighbors. She whispered a greeting to Anna Hartley, who was carefully arranging some potatoes and jars of strawberry jam.

Anna stopped her task to ask, "How's your garden?"

Sara cringed. She overharvested some of her early bloomers and forgot to cover others even though she was warned about an unusually late frost. Anna smiled and put up a hand. "Say no more. I'll come by."

"You're a gift, Anna! Thank you."

Sara and Bethany entered the council chamber where the elders were seated at a large round table speaking to one another in hushed tones. None of the elders seemed to notice they'd entered the room.

In front of two empty chairs sat a small plate with bread, cheese, and honey. It was enough to keep Sara's increasing annoyance at bay and hold her over until she got home.

Sara retrieved her record-keeping tools and slid into her usual seat. Bethany was already seated and digging into her food. The elders remained oblivious, continuing their conversation as though they hadn't summoned the women to this *urgent* meeting.

Bethany took a sip of ale and shot Sara a questioning look. Sara replied with a shrug and prepared to address the elders as soon as she finished chewing. Instead, Bethany set down her cup with enough force for the sound to echo through the chamber but not enough to break it.

Startled out of their discussions, the elders turned their attention to the women.

"My apologies, Councilors," Bethany said with a phony smile.

Sara gulped from her own cup to suppress her laughter.

"Good evening, Sara. Bethany. Thank you for joining us," Elder Councilor Tabitha Arden greeted with a slight bow. Her long white hair was pulled away from her face in a tight braided bun on the top of her head that barely moved with the gesture.

"I'm sure you must be tired from your travels to Willow Ridge. This shouldn't take long. We only wish to find out what you learned about John Dawson's illness and any news regarding the Commarasi."

"One moment, Elder Councilor." Councilor Thomas George raised a knotted pale finger. "Sara, what is that you're doing?"

Sara looked up from her ledger. The elders stared at her with unfamiliar intensity. "Recording the meeting. As I always do."

"This isn't an official matter, Sara," said Councilor George with a hint of condescension in his tone. "There's no need for a record."

"I think what little we've learned should be recorded so it can be referenced in the future if needed," Sara insisted.

Elder Councilor Arden cleared her throat. She smiled, but it didn't reach her cloudy blue eyes. "Why don't you share with us what information you've collected, and we'll determine if you need to provide a written account."

Sara didn't like this compromise. She'd never been asked to hold off taking an official record, and she resented the extra work it would require following the meeting.

"I'll start." Bethany pointed to Sara's dish, motioning for Sara to continue eating.

"I consulted with elder healing doulas and several of the Willow Ridge Council of Nine. None could recall a time when this specific illness had presented itself. They could speak to similar symptoms, but nothing so closely matching to what John Dawson is experiencing. They have heard rumors of some cases in the north of Valen, but since no one in Willow Ridge is currently suffering from this illness, their priorities lie elsewhere, and they've not sought confirmation. They've given me their word that they will share anything they learn."

Councilor George furrowed his brow, deepening the wrinkles. "What are their priorities?"

"Assisting nearby Amora villages that are at risk of a Commarasi takeover."

Councilor George leaned forward, crossing his slender arms on the table. "How?"

Sara stifled a frustrated sigh. Councilor George often asked people questions instead of making an effort to seek answers for himself.

"I was not given details, nor did I ask," Bethany said. "But Willow Ridge has always aided neighboring villages who have come on hard times. I can only assume Willow Ridge is expanding its reach so these villages don't become vulnerable to the Commarasi's propaganda."

"Anything else?" Elder Councilor Arden asked.

"Much like our animal keepers, the ferrymen are seeing unusually aggressive behavior from Teremedi sea creatures," Sara answered. "It's already impacting travel between Belhaven and the mainland and may begin to affect trade as well."

A heavy silence fell over the council. It only lasted a few heartbeats, but to Sara, it felt like an eternity. She wasn't accustomed to this kind of attention and scrutiny from the village leadership.

"With respect," Bethany began, her voice laced with impatience, "if you have no other questions for us, Sara must return to her children, and I must return to the Dawson home."

"Yes, Bethany. You're both dismissed," Elder Councilor Arden said with a wave of her hand.

"And the written record?" Sara pointed at her ledger.

"That won't be necessary, Sara," said Councilor George. "Also, I think it would be best if you kept this information to yourselves."

"What?" Sara exclaimed. "Why?"

"Because you've brought us mostly rumor and little has been verified," he said sharply. "Our people get enough of that from the bards. We don't need to add to their anxiety. Panic on our little island would be disastrous."

"I still think keeping track…" Sara began but was abruptly cut off by Councilor George.

"Sara Cortese!" Councilor George was irate now, and Sara flinched at the anger with which her name was said.

"You have a duty to this council, and this council has spoken. You will not create a written account of your trip to Willow Ridge, and you will not speak of unconfirmed information to the people of this village."

Sara stiffened, stunned into silence. She'd never been reprimanded like that, and her body throbbed with anger, embarrassment, and shame. Tears collected in the corners of her eyes, and she willed them not to fall.

Bethany pulled Sara from her seat and rushed them through the temple.

"What the fuck was that all about!" Sara yelled once they were on the other side of the village square. Sara paced in small circles and shook her hands to relieve the energy building up inside her.

"That's why they wanted to speak with us right away. They wanted to get our account before we spoke to anyone else so they could silence us!"

"He's an ass," Bethany said matter-of-factly. "But he's also not entirely wrong."

Sara stopped pacing and shot Bethany a look.

Bethany slowly stepped forward and took Sara's hand. Sara felt the warmth of their magic flowing between them, easing the tightness in her chest, and diffusing the oncoming eruption.

"When people don't have complete stories, they fill in the blanks themselves," Bethany said calmly. "What we learned today is an incomplete story. The Amora have lived for generations with little conflict, and our people are frightened."

Sara considered Bethany's point.

"You're right that there needs to be a written record, and we shouldn't keep this from our people." Bethany dropped Sara's hands to cup her cheeks. "And he's right that doing so may cause people to panic."

Bethany guided Sara's lips up to hers. Sara sighed into the kiss. Bethany's mouth tasted of sweet honey that lingered on her tongue.

Sara reluctantly pulled away and touched her forehead to Bethany's. "I want you," Sara whispered. "But John Dawson needs you."

Bethany kissed Sara's forehead, then her mouth, and wished Sara a goodnight.

When Sara arrived home, she found Stephen reading by the fire. Their two girls, Eleanor and Helen—who prefers to be called Lenni—were sound asleep on the rug, their bodies cocooned in blankets. Though they were both teenagers, for a moment, Sara expected to see toddlers nestled in those linens. They looked so small. Safe.

Sara stepped over them and kissed their father on the cheek.

"I made stew," Stephen whispered. "How was your mainland visit?"

Sara sighed with relief that she wouldn't have to prepare a meal for herself. "I need a little time to myself and then I'll fill you in. And you can explain what's going on here."

Sara moved quietly through the small kitchen, preparing herself a bowl of Stephen's venison stew. The heavy meal in her belly eased most of her remaining anger, turning it into simmering irritation. She drew in her journal as she ate, adding scenes of Willow Ridge to her catalogue.

Stephen walked into the kitchen and ladled himself a cup of stock. "Can I get you a cup?" he asked after setting his on the table across from Sara.

"If you wouldn't mind," she replied. She craved the feeling of something warm in her hands. "What's going on with the kids?"

Stephen sighed with a mix of frustration and concern that was uniquely his. "During lessons, they heard that their friend Rosalee wandered from her bed after hearing voices beckoning her to the woods. Her older brother was tending to a sick cow when he saw her heading into the forest."

"That's terrifying!" Sara cried. "Is Rosalee alright?"

"She's fine, but once she spoke out, a few other children said they also heard the voices. Most were stopped by their parents before they left their homes. So the girls are afraid to sleep alone. And in the dark."

Sara slumped in her seat. "And Louis?"

"He said if he hears any voices he'll tell them to '*shut up! I'm trying to sleep!*' and then went to bed."

Sara snorted. That sure sounded like Louis.

"Tell me about Willow Ridge," Stephen urged.

Sara suspected it was to keep her mind off her newfound worry for her children. And it would have if it didn't seem connected to the theory that malevolent creatures were passing through the rift and into their world.

Sara recounted the events in Willow Ridge with more detail than she and Bethany provided the council. She left out her salacious adventure with Bethany in the library. Sara and Stephen shared many things with each other, but those kinds of details were kept to themselves.

Her annoyance returned when she told him about her meeting with the elders. He leaned in, his features remaining mostly neutral. But Sara had known him for so long that she could see the shifting emotions in his dark eyes even without their magic tying them together.

"I'm so overwhelmed by it all," Sara said, her chest feeling like it could burst. "And I just don't know what to do anymore."

Stephen stretched his arm across the table and wiggled his fingers until she giggled and reached forward to hold his hand. Then he squeezed it three times.

I. Love. You.

It was a comforting gesture that spanned their shared life together and one they introduced to their children. Stephen wrapped his other large hand around Sara's, and the gratitude for his unwavering support escaped as tears in the corners of her eyes.

"Your duty to this village," he said, "is to preserve our history and traditions so that our descendants will be able to look to the past for guidance."

Remembering Maryanne's words, Sara's tears rolled down her cheeks, making small puddles on the wooden table. Sara swore an oath to her people, and she refused to break it.

Chapter 10

Bethany

Bethany woke with a start. She'd fallen asleep at the table next to a half-eaten pastry.

"She lives!" Piper rubbed soothing circles on her back as the sleep cleared from Bethany's eyes.

"I was starting to think you were dead." Piper laughed. She walked away to pour herself a cup of tea.

Bethany rubbed her face. Now that her mind knew everything was okay, her body tried to ease back into her nap.

Piper placed a cup of tea in front of Bethany, walked away, and returned with a fresh pastry. "Eat. Then leave," Piper said simply.

Bethany nearly choked on her tea. She'd never been sent away from a family, but John Dawson's case had exhausted her beyond comprehension. She didn't even have the energy to fight for her job.

"You need to take a day to yourself," Piper clarified. "Clearly, you need to sleep, but you need some joy too."

"I know, but," Bethany argued.

Piper leaned in and spoke quietly. "You and I both know that my father will begin his journey to the Goddesses any day now. Whatever ails him can't be cured and all I ask is that you make him as comfortable as possible until his journey begins."

Bethany's tears often fell in private, but she was too weary to keep them at bay. "I tried so hard, Piper," Bethany whispered, the words catching in her throat.

Piper wrapped her long arms around Bethany's shoulders and squeezed her tightly. "I know. This village needs you and your gift, and it would be selfish of me to let you wither away to nothing when I know in my heart that there is no saving him."

Bethany took a gasping breath and allowed more tears to fall. She marveled at the young woman who was already wise and compassionate beyond her years.

"Besides, the summer feast is tomorrow, and I think today is the perfect day to give this to Sara." Piper placed a small leather pouch on the table and slid it toward Bethany.

Bethany stared at it, her eyes still blurry with tears and exhaustion. She wiped them with her apron until she could see the pouch clearly. She picked it up, untied the lacing, and turned it over until a stunning gemstone necklace slipped into her hand.

It was more perfect than she ever imagined. "How did you know I was having this made for Sara?"

"I didn't, but you just confirmed my hunch." Piper leaned back in her chair and pumped her hands in the air in celebration.

"You tricky wench," Bethany said with a smile. "But wait, how'd you get this? Catrina Boudin was supposed to send for me when it was ready."

Bethany didn't think Piper's smile could get any larger. "Who do you think Catrina sources her jewelry wire from?"

Bethany rolled her eyes. Her friend was insufferable.

"Catrina had some very specific instructions, and I was curious how the piece came out. When she mentioned it was for you, I bribed her to entrust me with it so I could surprise you."

"Well, Catrina is a tricky wench too."

Piper's cackling laugh sent vibrations of happiness through the room and deep into Bethany's bones. In her short time in Belhaven, she'd come to know the most wonderful souls, and her heart was filled with gratitude.

The door to the Cortese family home was wide open when Bethany arrived. She stepped inside and called out a hello.

Stephen's disembodied voice responded. "Come to the kitchen, Bethany!"

Bethany found Stephen covered in flour and his hands expertly working a lump of dough. He was a beautiful man, who, by all accounts, was also a loving father and incredible partner. Adding the ability to make delicious baked goods made him more attractive.

"Sara is out in the garden," he said as he continued to knead. "Anna came by to give Sara's plants a little boost after she nearly killed them. What are you up to?"

"Piper kicked me out of the house for the day. I thought Sara might want to spend the day with me, but if she's busy." Bethany trailed off, mesmerized by the way Stephen worked the dough.

Stephen's woodworking magic seemed to make him incredibly gifted with his hands. He could build anything regardless of the material, and bread dough was just another material. He added a little oil to the round loaf and spread it over the surface with a gentle hand. Bethany felt her cheeks flush.

"Sara is never too busy for the people she loves." Stephen winked and slid the bread into the fire.

Bethany's whole body felt aflame as though she'd been tossed into the oven with the loaf. "Did she tell you that?" she whispered.

"She didn't need to." Stephen tilted his head toward the back door to urge her on.

Bethany stepped outside and found Sara standing in the middle of her sparse garden, while Anna, a verdant mage, kneeled over a sad-looking plant that Bethany didn't recognize. Anna ran her hands through the dirt around the plant, her magic dripping like spring rain from her fingertips and seeping into the soil.

"I wasn't aware that Stephen's bread-making technique was so ..." Bethany began.

"Seductive?" Anna finished, standing up straight. She dusted off her hands, her beige skin darkened by dirt and sun.

"Yes! That's exactly how I'd describe it," Bethany replied.

"I tease him mercilessly about it," Sara laughed. "Woodworkers are always so sensual with their materials."

Sara stroked Bethany's arm in an exaggerated manner, eliciting more giggles from the women.

"Well, maybe when he's done, you can send him my way," Anna said as she rebraided her long syrup-colored hair. "I'll put his sensual hands to work making maypop jam for the next supply run to Valen."

"When is that?" Bethany asked.

"Tomorrow evening," Anna replied.

Supply runs to the gatekeepers protecting vulnerable villages from the Commarasi had been increasing, and Bethany could no longer keep track of the collection schedule. It was only a few moons ago when she helped

Piper load armor into the collection carriage. The supply runs were the most reliable way to correspond with people in the field, and when she had enough notice, Bethany tried to send letters to Fredrick who would relay them to their daughter, Adessa.

"I'll have pain tonics and salves packed, and I'll bring them by," Sara added.

"It's less than usual given—" She gestured to the patch Anna had been working with. The spot was still bare, but the remaining plants had perked up a bit.

"Anything you share from your abundance is a blessing," Anna said.

Bethany gave Sara an encouraging smile.

"Especially if you happen to have an abundance of family members who can help with maypop jam." Anna winked.

Sara threw her head back in laughter so contagious that Bethany didn't dare hold back her giggles. "I'm sure Stephen and his sensual hands will be more than happy to assist."

When Anna had disappeared around the Cortese home, Bethany turned her attention back to Sara.

"So. Did Piper toss you out?" Sara asked with a knowing smile.

"She did, the brute. Said I needed joy and sunshine or some nonsense."

Sara took a few steps, closing the distance between them. "How dare she?" she said, playing into Bethany's teasing.

Bethany reached for the loose lock of hair that escaped from Sara's comb and twirled it around her finger. "I thought we might spend the day together."

"I was headed towards the sea today in search of more cattails," Sara replied. "If that's something that strikes your fancy."

"You strike my fancy, and I'd follow you into the forest or the sea anytime you ask."

Chapter II

Bethany

"This is my favorite tree in the whole forest," Sara said with an excited little jump. She pulled Bethany to a twisted oak tree. Its exposed roots snaked over large, weathered rocks, and its limbs dipped then climbed towards the sky.

The ocean was hidden from view, but the air was filled with salt and the familiar rhythm of crashing waves.

"I've concocted so many stories about what this ancient tree has seen during its life in this forest." Sara ran a hand over the bark and gazed at it with a familiar mix of wonder and curiosity.

Setting aside pouches of cattails and several other ingredients they'd harvested from the sands, Bethany shook a blanket loose from Sara's satchel and spread it out at the base of the tree.

"Tell me one." Bethany pulled Sara to the ground until they were snuggled in a nook made by the sprawling roots.

Bethany combed her fingers through Sara's hair while the scribe recounted her tales. Some were sad and others were silly. But they were all brilliant. Bethany wanted an entire library filled with Sara's brilliant stories.

"I have something for you," Bethany whispered against Sara's ear. "For the summer feast."

Sara gasped and shot up, spinning around to glare at Bethany. "I didn't know we were exchanging gifts!"

"We're not." Bethany stuck her tongue out at Sara. "Now close your eyes and open your hands."

Sara huffed but did as she was told.

Bethany gently dropped the quartz necklace into Sara's waiting hands. Her eyes popped open, and her jaw hung wide.

"Bethany!" Sara squealed. "This is fucking beautiful!"

Bethany watched Sara examine the necklace with the same wonder and curiosity that she looked at everything. Bethany wished she could freeze time so she could capture this look in a painting and keep it forever.

"A beautiful necklace for a beautiful woman," Bethany replied as she leaned in to kiss Sara's cheek.

"Not long after we met, we were working side-by-side overnight, and I don't recall what prompted it, but you said, *I wish I could put you in my pocket and take you everywhere with me.* And then you spent the rest of the night talking about how you'd fashion tiny things for me."

"Yes!" Sara cried. "I was so tired and just the mere thought of you being pocket-sized just had me in stitches."

Bethany took the necklace and clasped it around Sara's neck. "Well, I thought a necklace would be an acceptable alternative."

The quartz gemstones sparkled in the sunlight. It hung beautifully on Sara's chest, dipping below her freckled collarbone and resting just above where her pillowy breasts met.

"I would much rather have you by my side always, but yes, this will do." Sara winked. "Because a piece of me is missing when we're apart."

"You know why that is, right?" Bethany leaned forward until her forehead was touching Sara's, her stomach turning in lovesick knots.

"I have my theories." Sara bit her lip the way she always did to hold back a smile.

"We're soulmates," Bethany whispered.

"You think so?" Sara replied before stealing a few soft, chaste kisses.

"I know so." Bethany's exhaustion quickly dissipated as lust pumped through her body. "I knew it from the moment I felt our magic twist together like woodbine."

Bethany struggled against her body's screaming need to touch and taste Sara's every bit. But while Bethany rushed, Sara lingered. Both women often felt the pressure of being caregivers. Not just for their families but for the people in their community. Bethany coped by being driven by passion and led by lust. Sara, however, wanted to savor it all. She could make a few moments of pleasure feel like hours of ecstasy. They were perfectly balanced in that way.

Bethany pressed her fingers into Sara's fleshy hips, coaxing the other woman to straddle her thigh. Sara's lips left Bethany's mouth and trailed down the crook of her neck. Each kiss was soft and slow. Every light brush of Sara's tongue or scrape of her teeth was an unexpected burst of intensity that threatened to overtake her. Sara's patience taught Bethany that resisting her own wanton desire to fuck fast and hard fueled her pleasure.

Sara slowed to effortlessly remove Bethany's top, freeing her breasts from confinement. The air was hot, but the breeze danced over her skin, chilling her body. With her head thrown back, Bethany looked to the sky through the trees as Sara grazed her teeth and swept her tongue over Bethany's nipple. She indulged in every erotic sensation.

The rough stones of Sara's necklace scraped against Bethany's skin as she made a path of deep kisses back to Bethany's lips. Bethany's chest flushed with heat and radiated magic.

Amidst the kissing and the fondling, Sara rubbed herself against Bethany's thigh, her hips moving forward and back with increasing pressure. Sara's sexually generous nature meant she could get lost in making others feel good, and Bethany usually let Sara have her way. But for as much as she liked to tease and linger, Sara could also be greedy for pleasure, and Bethany relished those moments when Sara selfishly chased her own.

Gripping Sara's hips, Bethany lifted her leg to press her thigh into Sara's pussy. Sara broke their kiss and moaned softly against her mouth.

"That's it, love," Bethany cooed, keeping steady pressure as Sara rolled her hips in short, slow strokes.

Bethany reluctantly released her grip on the other woman so she could tear off Sara's bodice and tunic. The necklace caught the dappled sunlight and sparkled against Sara's lightly puckered chest. Bethany opened herself fully to Sara's magic, allowing her to see the way it glittered around Sara's undulating body like she too was made of quartz.

With one hand massaging Sara's breast and the other buried in her hair, Bethany trailed her tongue over Sara's glistening skin. Her lips lingered in the spot just under Sara's chin where her pulse raced. Bethany thanked the Goddesses for the ability to feel Sara's heart pounding harder with every thrust closer to bliss. Their hearts were beating in time when Sara cried out in ecstasy.

Overcome with a heady mix of emotion and lust, Bethany kissed Sara so fiercely that it brought their movements to a halt. And in that moment of stillness, Sara slipped her hand into Bethany's trousers. Bethany was wound so tight that the mere presence of Sara's fingers had her coming undone.

"*Fuck*," Bethany swore.

Sara laughed against Bethany's mouth but didn't stop toying with Bethany until she came twice more and they collapsed in a sated heap.

CHAPTER 12

SARA

Something felt off, but Sara couldn't put her finger on it. She stared into her cup of tea as though the answers would manifest in the bits of leaves that floated at the top.

"Mama?" said an insistent voice.

Sara barely heard her daughter over the thoughts rumbling through her mind. When she finally looked up from the cup, Eleanor stared at her with worry in her big brown eyes.

"I'm sorry, Sunflower, what did you need?"

At fourteen, Eleanor looked much less like her nickname than she did when it was given to her as a toddler. While her eyes were still pools of deep amber, her sunshine blonde hair had darkened as she grew. It was now closer in color to Sara's than to her father's.

"Nothing." Eleanor put down the bodice she was mending. "You look like something's bothering you, though."

"I have an ominous pit in my stomach, but I haven't a clue why." Sara sat back in her chair with a frustrated huff. She fiddled with her necklace, running her fingers over the stones' jagged edges. "I'm worried about Bethany."

"You should go to her then," Eleanor said. "You have plenty of time before nightfall, and Papa is here. Perhaps seeing her will ease your mind."

Sara rested her hand on top of her daughter's and squeezed it three times. "It probably would. Thank you, my Sunflower."

With her anxiety growing, Sara chose to ride her mare to the Dawson home instead of walking. She usually enjoyed the stroll, but today, speed was a higher priority. When Sara arrived, she led Zephyr into the stable near the family's workshop. Piper was taking violent swings with a heavy mallet as she hammered away at the hot metal of a broadsword.

Piper looked up and nodded at Sara before her mallet came down with a crash. Sara didn't wait for Piper to finish. The heavy weight of dread settled onto her shoulders and only worsened as she neared the house.

"Bethy?" she called, throwing John's bedroom door open. Her eyes scanned the room. John was on the bed, but flopped over on one side, as though he had tried to get up on his own but keeled over before standing.

Near John, she found Bethany in a heap on the floor next to the bed. Sara screamed out for Piper and rushed to Bethany's side. She lowered her cheek to Bethany's lips and listened. Her breath was so gentle Sara almost missed it. Sara ran to the door and yelled Piper's name, thankful the loud hammering had ceased. She tore through the kitchen looking for something that would revive her love.

Piper bounded through the door. "What's going on?"

"Bethany. I found her. Unconscious." Finding the oil she needed, Sara ran back into John's bedroom where he'd begun to stir.

Piper followed and tended to her father while Sara placed the open vial under Bethany's nose.

"Bethany!" Sara slapped Bethany's cheek with insistent force. "C'mon, Bethy! I need you to wake up for me."

Sara was prepared to throw Bethany into the icy ocean to shock the woman awake. Sara heaved a sob of relief when Bethany's eyes fluttered open and thanked the Goddesses between planting kisses across her face.

"Bethany, did my father attack you again?" Piper asked as she tucked the old man back under the covers.

As far as Sara knew, John had become much too weak to inflict pain upon a butterfly, let alone attack a woman of better health.

"No, I don't think so." Bethany struggled to sit up. "I don't remember what happened."

Sara pressed her lips to Bethany's temples. "Are you feeling ill? Your skin is quite chilled."

"I'm a bit sore from the fall. And tired. And confused. But I don't feel ill."

"You should come home with me so I can keep an eye on you," Sara said.

"That's fucking stupid," Bethany scoffed with unusual harshness. "I need to take care of John."

Too stunned to speak, Sara helped Bethany up from the floor. Bethany straightened her clothing and headed towards the kitchen.

Sara was taking a step to follow when Piper called, "Sara, wait."

She was momentarily torn between the two but turned towards the bed.

"My father is warm," Piper said.

It took a few beats for Sara to process what Piper was saying. "Warm?"

She placed the back of her hand on John's forehead and nearly gasped. He'd been so cold for so long, and now there was warmth. Though his face was still gaunt, some of the richness had returned to his brown skin. Sara wanted to celebrate this drastic improvement in John's condition, but couldn't until she checked on Bethany.

She left Piper with her father and found Bethany buzzing around the small room on unsteady legs, preparing a cup of tea. Sara returned the oil to its place and moved to a spot out of Bethany's path.

"Can I make something for you?" Sara asked gently.

"I'm fine," was her curt reply.

Piper joined them and like Sara, took up a place in the kitchen that was out of Bethany's way.

"Bethany, I haven't seen him rest this quietly in months," Piper said. "I can handle it. Go. You need to rest, and you can't do it here."

Bethany continued to protest but ultimately gave in to Sara and Piper's demands. With Bethany atop Sara's mare, they made most of the short journey back to the Cortese home in silence. The immediate relief Sara felt after Bethany opened her eyes had dissolved to unease. While the trepidation subsided, things still didn't feel quite right.

"I'm sorry I snapped at you," Bethany said, her eyes trained on Zephyr's silky mane instead of meeting Sara's. "I'll be so relieved when he's dead."

The harshness of her tone was more surprising to Sara than the words themselves.

"Isn't that awful of me?" Bethany mused. "To look forward to John Dawson's death? So I can finally rest and not be wracked with guilt that I can't fix him. I think I'd rather live with feeling shame than failure."

Sara stopped, her horse pausing beside her. She took Bethany's hand and gave it a little shake until Bethany looked down at her with somber eyes.

"You didn't fail, Bethy. The Goddesses did not make us to be immortal. You of all people should know that some afflictions can't be cured. Your responsibility to your patient then is to minimize their suffering so they leave this world peacefully."

"I've never seen a man suffer like John has," she spat.

"And he would have suffered even more if not for you. You are entitled to feel your emotions, Bethany Clement, but I will not allow you to speak of yourself with such disrespect."

Bethany replied with a heavy sigh. Sara released her hand, and Bethany averted her gaze once more. Needing a bit of comfort herself, Sara stroked Zephyr's neck before continuing the short journey home, dragging a heavy cloud of worry behind them.

CHAPTER 13

BETHANY

John will die today, Bethany thought.

She always knew when her patients were inching closer to the veil. It was a sad, but familiar, realization. This time, though, it was especially devastating because if not for the damage done to John's body, he might have made a full recovery.

Bethany rubbed some pain-relieving balm on her temples as she reread the notes in her patient journal. John's condition improved within a day of her falling unconscious at his bedside. The worst of his pain subsided, and he rested without the torture of vivid nightmares. The warmth returned to his skin, no longer feeling ice cold to the touch. Even his humor returned some. But his body had reached a point from which it couldn't return, and it was time for his spirit to move forward.

Bethany still had no memory of what triggered the collapse. Perhaps she used a near-lethal amount of her magic, and that's what it took to finally cure his illness. She scoffed to herself. Figures she'd have to nearly kill herself.

And for nothing, it seemed.

She shook the bitterness away. It wasn't for nothing. With his suffering no longer visible, Piper left to fetch her mother and siblings so they could spend time with John before he began his journey to Terultimi.

She closed the book and inspected the stew warming on the fire.

"I brought you something to eat, John," Bethany said as she placed a bowl of stew on the seat of the chair next to his bed.

He opened his eyes and smiled. "How about some mead to wash it down with?"

Bethany smiled and didn't argue. He'd get whatever he'd like today. When she returned with a glass and an unopened bottle, John was staring out the window with the bowl resting in his lap.

"I'm sorry, Bethany," he said without looking away.

"What on earth do you have to be sorry to me about?" Bethany asked and held out a full glass of mead.

He took the glass using both of his frail hands. His light brown skin was similar in color to Piper's, but months of illness had dulled its glow.

"The way I treated you these past weeks. Months? I don't even know how long it's been. I don't remember much, but I remember saying some horrid things to you."

Bethany laughed to ease the uncomfortable tension. "Yes, but I've been treated worse," she lied and smiled to sell it.

"But you are one of the few to apologize afterwards." That was the truth, however.

"I hope that's the thing you remember about me." John held up his glass in a weak salute and took a long sip.

She would. She'd also remember the kindness she now saw in his dark, round eyes and the way one side of his mouth lifted higher than the other when he smiled.

"What do you remember?" Bethany asked.

John stared at his stew, turning the thick vegetables around in the broth. "If I wasn't so close to death, I'd never admit any of this, but I remember a voice. Mine but cruel."

Intrigued, Bethany sat forward in her chair. "What did it say?"

John groaned and closed his eyes as though he could find his memories in the darkness. "It's fleeting," he said finally. "Like a dream after you wake. I remember its cruelty and its taunting but not its words."

Bethany let John eat a few spoonfuls of soup before speaking again.

"I've had several patients experience voices and see things that weren't there," Bethany said. "But they were hot with fevers. Your skin was like ice. Did you feel cold?"

"I felt the icy cold, but I wasn't cold," John said.

Bethany tilted her head, not understanding his words.

John sighed a laugh. "I wish I had the words to describe it. I imagine it's what a sentient puppet might feel like. I was simply an observer of my voice and my body instead of the one in control. And it became harder and harder to retake control until I just ... couldn't."

Bethany chewed on John's words while he ate, but no new ideas about his ailment manifested. Hallucinations weren't common, but they weren't abnormal for someone as ill as John. "Finish eating and get some rest. Your family will be home soon."

Bethany stood up, but John grabbed her hand. "Thank you, Bethany. For your care. Your spirit flows through your magic, and it was often my only anchor to this world. Without it, I wouldn't have been able to fight for as long as I did."

Bethany blinked away the tears that had clouded her vision and allowed them to roll down her cheeks. John had been so open with her, and she owed him this moment of her own vulnerability.

"Blessed journey, John."

Chapter 14

Bethany

Unless she was easing a patient into death or they'd be otherwise alone, Bethany never stayed for their final breaths. John Dawson was no different. He was comfortable, and he'd die without pain, surrounded by the people he loved most.

She often took this time for herself, walking aimlessly until her internal compass told her to stop. With her palms connected to the earth, she'd send her magic into the ground, taking with it all the pain and suffering to be filtered by nature and returned clear so she had the energy to do it all again for someone else.

She still needed all of that, but she didn't want to be alone. Despite John's words, Bethany had difficulty acknowledging that anything she'd done made a difference. Self-doubt began its slow creep up her spine, and she needed Sara to scare it away.

Sara was at the temple, seated at the familiar circular table, her quill flying across the page as an Amora villager spoke with a voice heavy with worry. Bethany hadn't met him yet, but his angular face and short stature were familiar so they must have crossed paths at some point. She anticipated meeting more villagers now that John Dawson wouldn't be her only charge.

"This is the third hog I've found in bloody pieces since the last full moon," the man said, raising three slender fingers to emphasize his point. "My magic is not like that of our farmers. I can't make my livestock mature more quickly. If we continue like this, it will impact Belhaven's food supply."

"And you're sure it's not the red wolves?" asked Councilor Thomas George, the slight raise of one bushy eyebrow suggested he wouldn't believe him regardless. "Others have said they've been unusually bold of late."

The small man released an exasperated sigh, and Bethany caught Sara biting her lip to hold back a smile as she wrote.

"Forest creatures may not be my specialty, but anyone who spends as much time with animals as I do would know this is not the work of wolves." The feisty man leaned forward and addressed Councilor George directly.

"The wolves only hunt when they're hungry, consuming most of their kill and what is left is feasted on by vultures. Whatever maimed this hog didn't eat it. Just tore it to shreds." He curled his fingers and mimed pulling something apart.

"And just like the last, the vultures haven't touched it. Nothing has touched it. Not even the flies."

The elders sat in silence around their large circular table, the scratching of Sara's quill the only sound echoing through the space.

"And before you ask," he continued, "it wasn't a cougar either."

Sara snorted, earning a harsh look from several councilors. Bethany couldn't imagine sitting through these meetings for hours on end the way Sara did.

"I think we may have a santer in our realm," said Councilor Lavina Charlie as she leaned forward in her seat.

She wasn't much older than Bethany, making her the youngest elder on the council. Bethany knew her the best of the nine, but that wasn't saying much since she didn't know any of them very well.

"They usually pass through the gates near the mountains and feed on livestock. Belhaven would be an unusual hunting ground for them, but I don't know of any earthly creature that could do this," Councilor Charlie continued. "Who is guarding the gate?"

"Ophelia Yates and her cousins," answered another. Bethany struggled to remember their name. "But they only recently returned from fighting the Commarasi in Valen. The rift went unguarded for several moon phases before that."

"I'm empathetic to the plight of our Amora family on the mainland," Councilor Charlie said. "But if more sinister creatures are passing into our realm, we must be more discerning as to how many gatekeepers we send to assist their battles."

Elder Councilor Tabitha Arden sighed heavily and put up a hand to hush the chatter. "We'll cross that bridge when we get there. Let's rest for a bit before we continue."

The council nodded in agreement and relaxed in their seats or stood to leave the room or speak with others. When she finished writing, Sara jumped from her seat and crossed the room.

"Did John?" Sara said quietly when she reached Bethany. There was no reason for her to finish the sentence.

Bethany nodded. "Not yet, but soon. I still feel the presence of his spirit, but it's weak."

Sara's eyes widened with surprise. "All the way from here?"

"Thankfully, I only know that he's still in his corporal body, not what he's doing with it." Bethany winked.

Sara laughed, her eyes sparkling in the candlelight. Bethany appreciated Sara's easy humor during these sad times. Few seemed to understand Bethany's need to use laughter to process solemn moments.

"And you chose to spend your free time here?" Sara whispered.

"You're here, soulmate." Bethany leaned forward and kissed the tip of Sara's nose.

Sara flinched and wiggled her nose.

"What was that?" Bethany asked.

"What was what?"

"You flinched when I kissed your nose. Did you not like it?"

Sara's features twisted into genuine confusion. "I … don't know. I don't remember doing anything."

"Nevermind," Bethany said. Though it felt like something, it was probably nothing, and she changed the subject.

They caught up quietly until the elders returned and called the meeting to order. The brief time together was a breath of fresh air, and Bethany wanted to inhale more of Sara's sweetness.

The meeting continued. More villagers aired their concerns, some speaking directly of John's illness. Bethany remained quiet in the back of the chamber. The Dawsons never gave her permission to share his prognosis publicly, and she wouldn't unless she suspected the village was in danger. Whatever ailed him didn't seem to be easily transferred to others.

The elders discussed a more thorough investigation, and Bethany scoffed silently and rolled her eyes. As though any of these people could do more thorough research than

Bethany and Sara already had. If they could, they should have done it already, she thought. Investigations of this nature never amounted to anything other than providing someone to blame.

And that someone was usually the healing doula.

CHAPTER 15

SARA

Sara adjusted the basket on her arm. It hung heavier than its true weight. It held fresh fruits, a loaf of bread, several balms, and all of Sara's dread over this visit with Bethany.

Being in Bethany's presence used to bring Sara warmth and comfort, but much had changed in the two months since John left the mortal plane. It was subtle at first. A slight discomfort accompanied Bethany's cool touch. A hostile edge to her tone came next and gloom with it. It all worsened from there.

Every day, Sara's heart broke further with the struggle of being in her lover's company. It was a duality of emotions that she couldn't process. Being near Bethany brought a despair she never before experienced. The misery was a wet blanket smothering her until she left the building.

But Sara couldn't stay away. Her magic wanted to run, but never too far. As amorous soulmates, they were destined to spend their lives together. The exhausting push and pull of these emotions only added more dread to the basket she held.

Sara took a deep breath and walked into the tavern. It was emptier than usual at this time in the evening. The village was experiencing its own duality. It was quiet and far too loud. Less people were out, opting to remain in the perceived safety of their homes. But their magic, their energy, and their movements always felt on the verge of panic.

Most were cautious.

A few were paranoid.

More villagers were asking Sara for larger batches of her wares so that they wouldn't need to call on her as often. Some went as far as asking how they were made so they could provide for themselves. She reminded them that without her specific magic, anything they prepared wouldn't have the same potency. A few wanted to know anyway, and she provided them with some basic recipes.

Jameson, the tavern owner, waved Sara over with a stony expression.

"How is she?" Sara asked.

"No better. Probably worse, if I'm being honest."

Sara rubbed her face with her free hand. She hadn't felt this exhausted since her children were the size of summer melons and screamed or fed through the night. Now they sleep, but she and Stephen stay awake taking shifts to ensure nothing lured them from their beds.

"People are whispering about her," Jameson said quietly. "Wanting to know why they can't call on her and if she has the same disease that killed John Dawson. I'm curious myself. I don't mind giving her the room while she's caring for the village, but if she's sick, I don't want my other tenants catching it."

In the beginning, Sara defended Bethany with confident ferocity. John's illness was nothing that either of them had ever encountered and required more magic and more of Bethany's life force than should ever be expected of a healer. Of course it would take time for her body to recover.

And the villagers believed it. Because Sara believed it.

But Sara didn't believe it anymore.

"She wouldn't put you or your tenants in danger, Jameson."

He arched a manicured brow. "So she is ill."

Sara threw her head back with an irritated groan. "I know little more than you."

She pulled a small vial from the basket and placed it on the bar between them.

"Ahh. Splendid." Jameson picked it up, slipping it into the inside pocket of his vest. "My partners have been very satisfied."

Too tired to continue the conversation, Sara turned to leave and trudged up the steep wooden stairs that led to the tenant rooms. Bethany's was at the end of the hall. A corner room with big windows and a view of the sea bought with the tonic that Sara just delivered. She thought the light and sea air would hasten Bethany's recovery, but during her last visit, she found the curtains drawn shut and the room cast in darkness.

Sara knocked, then tried the doorknob. When it turned easily, she inched the door open, once again finding a dark room. Bethany was tucked in a corner on the floor, her head resting on her kneecaps. Though not yet frail, Bethany had shrunk in size, her delicious curves melting off her body overnight.

"Hello, Bethy," Sara said gently.

Bethany picked up her head, and Sara could have been looking at a ghost. Dark circles made rings around her hollow green eyes, and her once-gentle wrinkles deepened. Her brown hair was almost completely white, the curls flat, and the texture brittle like straw.

"My love." Bethany smiled weakly and pulled Sara down for a kiss. Sara shuddered when Bethany's icy lips touched hers. They were so cold they should have been deep blue instead of the pale pink they'd turned.

The cold was shocking, but it was the next sensation that caused her to recoil. Bethany parted Sara's lips with her tongue to deepen their kiss. No matter how Sara adjusted her breath, every exhale felt pulled from her body. Not just the air sucked from her lungs, but the magic deep inside her bones.

Panic began to rise in her chest, and she fought the urge to shove Bethany away. Sara broke their embrace and got up before Bethany could reach for her again.

"Why so much darkness, Bethy?" Sara flung open the curtains, flooding the room with sunshine. Bethany covered her eyes.

"I like it," she hissed.

Sara's composure slipped. "You know who also liked darkness before he died? John fucking Dawson."

Bethany stood up quickly, but the jolt of energy didn't last long, and she put her hand on a nearby dresser to brace herself.

"Lots of people like darkness when they're ill, Sara. Or tired. Or completely empty of the energy that keeps them alive."

"But they also don't have nightmares keeping them awake." Sara insisted, her voice becoming louder. "Their skin isn't as cold as the winter ocean."

Bethany sat on the bed with a childlike huff. "This is normal for what I've been through, Sara. You don't understand because you use plants to heal. Not your body. You're not sacrificing anything."

Bethany's words were quiet but sharp, her tone almost unrecognizable. Sara stood motionless as she cycled through a range of emotions: anger, confusion, heartbreak.

"This isn't normal!" Sara screamed. "It's been months! Nothing about this is normal!"

She didn't know what else to say after that, and in the silence she felt her magic trying to flee. She usually fought it, but this time she couldn't. She was too heartbroken and angry to do anything else but walk away.

CHAPTER 16

SARA

Sara stared at the nearly empty page in front of her. The Council of Nine began the day's meeting at the height of the midday sun to debate the merits of sending more gatekeepers to vulnerable Amoran villages across Arcanos. There would be little details of those merits, however. Sara struggled to focus and translate the conversation from spoken word to written record.

The gist of it seemed to be that though Belhaven was a relatively small community, the presence of a rift on the island meant they had more trained fighters than villages located further away. But that also made them more vulnerable to evil spirits and creatures that could pass through. The elders went round and round having the same conversations each day. Sara didn't know the right answer, but the time spent at the table was taking her away from her family and her alchemist work.

It did give her a reason to avoid Bethany, and for that she felt the most shame. Her encounter with Bethany the previous day added worry to the mix, and she was wracked with guilt for walking away.

A bell chimed, shocking Sara out of her trance in time to record the vote taking place. The elders overwhelmingly agreed, but on what, Sara wasn't sure. She missed the motion and would have to fill in that information later.

"Next we'll hear from Bethany Clement, village healing doula," said Elder Councilor Tabitha Arden.

Sara came alive and jumped up from her seat, adrenaline shooting through her body. She watched in horror as Bethany was led into the room by a council guard. The guard escorted her to an empty seat at the round table that happened to be almost directly across from Sara.

"Do you think it's appropriate for Scribe Cortese to take the official record of our questioning?" asked Councilor Thomas George. "As they have a personal relationship."

She hadn't noticed she was still standing, but she was empowered by her relative height. Sara picked up her ledger. "These records are filled with people I have personal relationships with," she spat.

"I trust that Scribe Cortese will create an accurate record of our meeting." Elder Councilor Arden gave her a stern look. "She's never given us a reason to presume otherwise."

That's a lie, Sara thought.

The elders hadn't asked her outright to record any untruths, but there were many lies of omission. The records may be considered accurate, but they were far from complete.

Sara bit her tongue and sat down, picking up her pen. Bethany's lackluster gaze flitted around the room.

"Healer Clement. Let's start from the beginning," continued Elder Councilor Arden.

Bethany painstakingly rehashed her account of John's illness. His symptoms, his treatment, and all the research Bethany and Sara had done in Willow Ridge. Sara jumped in where Bethany struggled to remember exact timelines and details. Many of which were likely in her patient journal, and Sara noted that Bethany arrived empty-handed.

When she was finished, Bethany slumped further into her seat like the whole testimony took a great deal of energy. She rubbed her temple in the same spot she complained of persistent pain. The spot was red and raw from her constant circling.

"Thank you for that, Healer Clement," said Councilor Thomas George without looking up from his papers.

"Now it's been two full moons since John Dawson began his journey to the Goddesses, and you have been unable to fulfill your duties to the people of this village. Healer Simon cannot sustain this work alone at their age, and their mentee has only just begun his training. I don't understand why the Goddesses would have given us two healers if the strongest of the pair refuses to work. Perhaps they were wrong in sending you."

It took all of Sara's self-control to keep from launching her glass at the old man's face, then crawling across the table to finish the job. His words were needlessly cruel, but he was right about Bethany being the strongest healer. Asa Simon was in their sixtieth year, and Bethany was meant to take on most of their load while Asa trained their mentee. The boy still had too much to learn to be responsible for the needs of an entire village.

Councilor Lavina Charlie picked up from there, her tone firm but her eyes soft. "The Goddesses don't make mistakes, Bethany. We know that your magic requires more of you than others, and we have always been patient as our doulas recover. But we have reason to believe that you're afflicted with the same illness that killed John Dawson and that's why you've stopped performing your official duties."

Sara stopped writing but kept her head down so no one would see the tears forming in the corners of her eyes. She wanted to defend Bethany, but she didn't. Maybe this was what Bethany needed to realize she wasn't okay.

"We cannot control what is happening beyond our borders, but we can control more deaths from this mysterious disease by separating its latest victim from our people," said Councilor George.

"What?" Sara gasped, staring hard at the old man, who refused to meet her eyes.

Sara looked at Bethany, who remained silent in her seat. Her expression was solid like stone, except for her eyes. They flashed with panic.

Why wasn't she fighting back? Sara thought. *Say something.*

Bethany opened her mouth, presumably to speak, but she only uttered a few unintelligible sounds.

Ignoring Sara, Elder Councilor Arden cleared her throat. "Healer Bethany Clement, you will be sequestered to the temple crypt while this council determines the most appropriate course of action."

"No!" Sara yelled, jumping up from her seat and slamming her hands on the table.

"Scribe Cortese, sit down and continue your duties," said Elder Councilor Arden, her tone icy.

"She's committed no crime!" Sara cried, thrusting a hand towards Bethany. "Yet you banish her to a dungeon? Never in our history have we done that because it's inhumane!"

Councilor Charlie snapped her fingers, drawing Sara's attention. "It is an unfortunate truth that Healer Clement poses a danger to the people of this village, and it's our responsibility to keep the village safe. Now sit down and continue *your* responsibility, Scribe Cortese, or we'll have you removed from these chambers."

Sara's gaze turned to Bethany who looked up at her with pleading eyes. Bethany gave a stiff nod, then looked away.

Sara fell into her seat and scrawled the motion in the book. Though she wasn't a member of the Council of Nine, Sara included her dissent.

Because it was her responsibility to record the truth.

CHAPTER 17

SARA

The temple crypt was a sacred space, but it was a space meant for the dead to rest. The living can't thrive without fresh air and light from the sun. Bethany was proof of that.

When Sara arrived, Bethany was lying on a cot in the corner of her cell, her body twitching aggressively as she acted out the nightmare that plagued her. Sara called out, but it wasn't enough to wake her. She was forced to wait it out; helpless to ease the pain and suffering her love endured.

Bethany woke with a gasp that lifted her body off the cot. Her eyes immediately trained on Sara's and smiled weakly with relief. Moments later, Bethany began to sob.

Sara fell to the ground and reached through the bars. "Bethy, it's okay. Come to me."

The boulder in Sara's stomach threatened to send her own tears streaming down her face, but she forced them back to remain calm in Bethany's presence. Bethany slid off the cot and crawled to the gate, collapsing the moment her frigid grip took hold of Sara's hand. Sara fought against the cold and the urge to flee to whisper soothing words while Bethany cried. She cried about the pain and the exhaustion and the nightmares that plagued her night and day.

"It's so loud," Bethany sputtered.

"What's so loud, love?"

"It. My mind. It's so loud."

Sara sighed, unsure what to say. When she first spoke of her mind being too loud, Sara asked gentle questions to gain more information. But Bethany never gave her any more than that.

Instead, she dabbed some ointment on Bethany's temples. The same ointment she prepared for John and used until it no longer worked. Sara's fingertips warmed as her magic fused with the mixture. It fought against the icy chill of Bethany's skin.

Bethany's sobs became a whimper and soon a sigh.

Sara wet a clean cloth with cleansing water and wiped Bethany's face and hands. The flowery scent filled the dark space, temporarily blocking out the smell of damp earth. By the time Sara was done, Bethany had calmed, and everything seemed to settle. Her breath, her body, and her magic.

Bethany's symptoms worsened dramatically once banished to the crypt. Sara hadn't realized it before, but living at the inn, surrounded by people that cared for her, had done much to slow the progression of Bethany's illness. But Sara knew that like John, Bethany would only get worse. It was hard enough watching him deteriorate. She couldn't bear even the thought of Bethany being on that same trajectory.

She couldn't let Bethany die in this cage.

The Council of Nine didn't begin discussing Bethany's fate until the end of their meeting. Sara worked quietly alongside her elders, but her notes were the barest interpretation of events. Her thoughts kept returning to Bethany and the way she looked huddled against the bars of her cell.

"Shall we finally discuss the most urgent matter at hand?" said Councilor Thomas George.

Sara stood up so quickly her chair tipped backwards and hit the floor with a crash that echoed through the chamber. "You must release Bethany Clement!"

"Sara, please!" scolded Councilor Lavina Charlie.

"She's only worsened since you banished her to the darkness!" Sara yelled. "The Goddesses do not permit us to purposely cause the suffering of our people, and yet that is what you do to our village healer!"

"She is a danger to our village!" Councilor George yelled back.

"How?" Sara demanded, crossing her arms. Their decision to keep Bethany sequestered in the crypt defied common logic, and she'd had enough.

"I have been with Bethany almost every day since she arrived in Belhaven and yet, I am fine. Piper Dawson has spent even more time with Bethany, and she's healthier than everyone sitting around this table."

Sara glared at each elder as they sat silently and evaded her burning gaze. Even Councilor George pressed his lips into a tight line.

"If she's such a danger, then why wasn't John Dawson locked away?" Sara challenged. "Why was he allowed freedom, but Bethany is such a danger she must be caged?"

Even though they didn't know the severity of John's illness then, Sara couldn't understand why Bethany was being treated so differently. Though they didn't happen frequently, Belhaven wasn't immune to serious illness. Its history included disease outbreaks that wiped out entire families. To Sara's knowledge, there'd never been a time when someone so ill was quarantined in such a heartless w ay.

"She's dying!" Sara screamed at them, her face flushed with anger. Tears threatened to fall, but she refused to let them.

"Which is why her spirit must be cleansed!" Elder Councilor Tabitha Arden yelled in response.

"What?" Sara whispered, her voice hoarse.

The rest of the elders looked away, the expressions on their faces unreadable.

"Bethany Clement will die," said Elder Councilor Arden with little sympathy in her voice. "And since we don't know the cause, her soul should be cleansed so that we ensure that she spends eternity with the Goddesses and her loved ones."

"A cleansing execution?" Sara seethed. "Are you fucking mad?"

"Sara Cortese, I've had enough of this," Councilor George slapped his hand on the table. "Your proximity to this council has caused you to believe that you may speak to us in such a disrespectful manner. You've been unable to meet your responsibilities as village scribe, and I motion to remove you from the position effective immediately."

Sara watched in stunned silence as the nine elders voted unanimously to strip her of her title. No scribe had ever been forcibly removed. Sara hadn't even been in the position long enough to name and train a successor. The council could keep their own records but without a neutral party, who was to say those accounts would be truthful?

A council assistant put his hand on Sara's shoulder, and it was only then that she realized they were also removing her from the meeting. She shook off the assistant's grip and turned on her heel. She walked swiftly through the temple and into the afternoon's waning sunlight, leaving the chambers as darkness fell.

ANNOUNCEMENT

From the Belhaven Council of Nine

Be it known that on the seventy-second day of summer, the Isle of Belhaven Council of Nine have come to the unanimous decision as to the fate of Amora Healing Doula Bethany Clement.

Healer Clement arrived on the Isle of Belhaven on the thirty-second day of spring to assist in the care of Metalworker John Dawson. Unable to determine the cause of his suffering, Metalworker Dawson succumbed to his illness and began his journey to Terultimi on the thirteenth day of summer.

Since then, Healer Clement has shown symptomatic evidence of the same terminal illness. For the protection of the community, the Council of Nine has determined a cleansing execution is the most appropriate course of action.

Healer Clement's spirit will be purified so that she may be able to pass through Teremedi and spend eternity with our

Goddesses.

We make this decision with grief in our hearts.

The ritual will begin in seven days at sunrise.

Elder Councilor Tabitha Arden

Councilor Thomas George
Councilor Lavina Charlie
Councilor Elani Blake
Councilor Clarina Akari
Councilor Ellen Chandler
Councilor Mateo Sidney
Councilor Silas Kacey
Councilor Issac Hollis

CHAPTER 18

BETHANY

Unable to witness the setting of the moon and the rising of the sun made it impossible for Bethany to know how close she was to death. Sara would know, but she hadn't seen her lover since the day the elders decided to murder her.

Or had she?

Bethany had no memory of Sara's visits, but the lack of memory didn't feel real.

The more she tried to recall, the louder her doubts became until she could hear the voice clearly between her ears.

You're all alone. No one is coming for you.

"No, I suppose not," Bethany replied aloud.

Not even your daughter. If she's even aware.

"Unlikely. I never got to tell Sara about Adessa."

Sara is untrustworthy and would have put Adessa in danger.

"I wish I could say goodbye."

Sorrow filled Bethany's chest, and she wanted to cry, but the tears wouldn't come.

Darkness came instead.

The torch flames glowed, but the shadows grew along the walls and spread through the crypt like fog rolling over the water. No longer holding back her magic, Bethany felt the spirits of two familiar people. The prison became dark as the new moon night, but Piper Dawson and Ophelia

Yates were clear as daylight as they approached Bethany's cell.

It finally occurred to her that Ophelia, a luminary, was using her magic to control the shadows. Bethany stood up, wavering with weakness, and stumbled towards the bars.

"What the fuck are you doing?" Bethany whispered.

Piper put her hands on the metal lock. "Committing several crimes. What does it look like we're doing?"

The heat of Piper's magic sizzled on Bethany's skin, a painful reminder of why she kept it on a short tether. After a few seconds that passed like hours, Piper pulled a small hammer from a pack on her hip and tapped the lock until it released. A metalworker—likely of Piper's family line—used their magic to strengthen the metal when the lock was forged. Piper now used that same magic to weaken it.

If you leave, the lives of the ones you love will be at risk. Their blood will be on your hands.

The gate creaked open, offering Bethany her escape, but she knew her freedom was a lie.

Chapter 19

Sara

An unrelenting summer rain fell on Belhaven.

Five days earlier, Sara stood in the village square as a council aide read a bulletin announcing Bethany's fate. She collapsed into Stephen's arms and wept until she had nothing left. When Sara's tears ran dry, tears from the sky took their place, and the heavens continued to cry on her behalf.

Sara spent as much time with Bethany as she could withstand. Not being able to physically tolerate being in Bethany's presence during their last days together in this realm brought Sara an indescribable amount of sorrow.

Bethany's magic rattled her nerves, making her short-tempered. Sara spent an infuriating amount of time during every visit convincing Bethany that she visited every day. Sara determined it was easier to apologize for not visiting. The lie prevented an argument, and fake apologies were less aggravating, allowing a bit more peace before Bethany was sentenced to the rarest of Amoran rituals.

Sara sat by the fire, mesmerized by the dancing flames. Beside her was a journal open to a blank page. She intended to record the events of the past few weeks, but she found it too painful and the words too hard to summon.

Eleanor came into the room balancing a teacup on a mismatched saucer.

"I made this for you, Mama," she said. "I think I finally perfected the energy and clarity spell."

Sara looked through the window into the darkness of the forest, then laughed. "Sunflower, energy and clarity is usually a daytime spell."

"Well, in my defense, it was daytime when I started preparing it," she replied with a precocious smile.

Sara took the cup and saucer from her daughter and examined the dark green liquid.

"It does take an obnoxiously long time to brew." Sara winked and took a sip.

The exhaustion she'd be sure to feel the next day was worth encouraging Eleanor to continue practicing and experimenting in order to keep this part of their family history alive. Magic didn't come easily for her oldest daughter, but she had a way of mixing spells with complementary herbs to enhance the flavor, so they were a treat to ingest even if they weren't as potent.

"This is delicious," Sara said after a few more long sips. "Tell me about how you made it."

Though genuinely curious, this was also part of the test. Eleanor spoke quickly, often skipping parts of her process, then jumping back to include what she missed. Her monologue sometimes veered off on tangents about everything she learned about a minor ingredient. If Sara could follow and comprehend everything her daughter said, then it was a success.

Eleanor was explaining her thought process for choosing wild bergamot instead of yarrow as the spell called for when there was a heavy and urgent knock at their door.

"Who would be visiting at this hour? In this weather?" Sara asked, putting her cup and saucer down and standing up. Her hand instinctively reached for the dagger on her hip.

Stephen jogged from the kitchen to open it without any hesitancy and seemed unsurprised by their late visitor.

"Piper?" Sara squinted at the tall, cloaked figure now standing in their home. "What's going on?"

Eleanor wrapped her birdlike arms around Sara as Stephen approached. "You need to go with Piper," he said. "She will take you to Bethany and get you both someplace safe."

Two more pairs of arms wrapped tightly around her body. Lenni and Louis.

"But I can't leave them," Sara whispered.

How could she leave her babies? How could any mother leave her babies behind to risk her life for someone else?

But that someone else was meant to be by her side always. A perfectly matched spirit, blessed by the Goddesses. The guilt of wanting to stay warred with the shame for wanting to leave.

"It's okay, Mama," Louis said. He'd grown so much over the winter that his big hazel eyes were now level with hers. His sweet voice carried a bit of depth and confidence. "Our family is big, and they'll care for us until you come back."

Stephen pulled the entire family into his long arms and rested his forehead on Sara's temple. His beard tickled the side of her face and caught her falling tears. "We know you'll return with our village's healer because only you possess the sheer will, stubborn determination, and magical ability to do so."

Despite the permission from her family, Sara's feet stayed planted, unable to move.

Lenni pulled away from the group and brushed her short blonde hair out of her eyes.

"We can't let the elders do this to our people, Ma," Lenni said firmly. She had Stephen's height, and at thirteen, she was already taller than Sara and Eleanor. She was normally quite reserved but knew how to use her stature to demand attention.

"Today it's Bethany. Who will be next?" Lenni said. "You're not leaving us. Your resistance will save us."

"Fuck." Sara let the tears fall but kept her composure. "I'd like my babies back when I return. No more of this growing you three are doing."

Sara kissed them all and squeezed them tightly, imprinting the pressure of their bodies onto her skin.

Piper handed Sara her cloak and her satchel. It was stuffed with clothing, medicine, and food. In the stable, Sara's mare Zephyr was saddled up to ride through the rain, her saddlebags stuffed with more supplies.

Everything was ready to go. Everyone was prepared for Sara's flight into the night. Even her daughter made her tea to give her the energy and focus she'd need.

They'd planned this, Sara realized.

They planned this for her and Bethany. Nothing would stop her from making the journey. She owed it to them.

The steady rain showed little mercy as Piper and Sara rode to Belhaven's north sea. The ride was tricky even in the best conditions, but a red fox guided their way. Getting to the harbor safely was more important than getting there quickly.

Once out of the shelter of the forest, Sara and Piper were met with strong winds that pelted them with coarse sand. The ocean waves crashed violently against the shore, mixing the salty spray with fresh rain.

As they neared the dock, she saw Catrina Boudin and Bethany illuminated by the lamplight. Sara flung herself off her horse and passed the reins to a waiting ferryman before running to Bethany. The other woman's heavy cloak swallowed her frail body. Bethany collapsed in Sara's arms and kissed her weakly. Bethany's face and lips were ice cold, and Sara yearned for Bethany's warm embrace.

"I promise you, Bethany Clement, I will bring heat back to your touch. I will save you."

Chapter 20

Sara

The Valley of Asters

Sara woke to a gentle tapping on the opposite side of the small bedroom. The crow perched outside the window was an obsidian silhouette against the predawn darkness. Sara groaned when it tapped again, irritated that this wake-up call was interrupting the best sleep she'd had in weeks.

Bethany's increasingly painful headaches and disrupted sleep had taken their toll, leaving Bethany temperamental and weak, and Sara with diminished patience. Since arriving nearly a fortnight ago, Sara spent most nights holding Bethany in her arms. The comfort didn't keep the nightmares at bay, but Bethany was easier to soothe when she woke in terror.

But Sara knew that if she wanted these restful nights to continue, she needed to get moving. Before slipping out of bed, Sara rubbed some balm on Bethany's forehead and the back of her neck. It was a new spell, concocted from the plants that grew around the cabin. Most could also be found on Belhaven, but some were new and better suited to live in the valley at the edge of the mountains in the north of Valen. Though it didn't cure Bethany of whatever ailed her, it offered her the most relief than anything they'd tried in months.

Bethany's smile returned first, then her laugh. Every giggle set fire to Sara's soul, pushing her forward when everything felt hopeless.

That morning, the air was crisp, and a change to the earth was coming with the arrival of the autumnal equinox. The mossy ground under Sara's feet was still warm, but the first fallen leaves began knitting their winter blanket. The sky turned amethyst, and the stars disappeared from the heavens.

"Blessed morning, pups," she said to the family of red wolves that slowly emerged from the forest.

Sara left them a small bowl of boiled eggs and overripe fruit near a mossy tree stump where a bowl of water sat. The nameless guides that brought Sara and Bethany to this place in the Valley of Asters told them little about the cabin other than it belonged to an animal keeper who entrusted the wolves and other animals with its protection. The wolves guarded the cabin all day and all night, but it was only in the morning before her ride to the Amora library of Sanctum Celestia that Sara ever saw them.

Zephyr was nestled in the barn she shared with a small flock of chickens, and Sara hated to disturb her sleepy mare even before the rooster woke. Every morning she wished for it to be her last ride so she could let the animal rest.

The journey to Sanctum Celestia was an unpredictable one. Despite having made it numerous times since her arrival in the valley, she wasn't confident she could get there on her own. Each day she was escorted by a flock of crows who followed the song of the chickadees leading them on the safest path.

Sara always sighed with relief when she passed under the Sanctum Celestia's stone archway. Though it was a sanctuary, there was no guarantee that Sara would be safe there. She was well aware that she committed a crime by aiding Bethany's escape, and the librarians were under no obligation to harbor a fugitive.

Even still, she felt safe inside the magnificent cathedral.

Sara's boots echoed through the stone tunnel that led to the wooden doors of the sacred library's entrance. She tried to quiet her rushed pace, but her visits always felt too short. The windows were made of a rainbow of colored glass, and it was easy to ignore the passage of time. There was less light each day, and Sara always promised Bethany she'd return by dusk.

Isolde Letsatsi sat at a heavy wooden desk behind a tower of thick books. The flowing sleeves of her pale-yellow librarian cloak were tied with ribbon above her elbows, keeping them out of her way as she used her left hand to make notes on a large piece of parchment.

She wasn't much older than Sara, but her work in one of their most sacred libraries gave her two lifetimes worth of knowledge. Sara expected that someone who spent so much time reading would be frail. But Isolde immediately put that expectation to rest as she walked briskly from one side of the library to the other, often taking two steps at a time to the upper levels, and returning with an armful of books that weighed more than toddlers.

"Those aren't for me, are they?" Sara asked.

Isolde smiled, deepening the gentle lines around her upturned hazel eyes. But she didn't reply until she finished making her notes.

"No, sadly not. But those are." Isolde pointed to a much smaller collection of books and scrolls on a nearby table.

"Allow me to finish this task and then I'll show you what I found."

Every visit filled her with a rush of optimism that made her belly twist. Within its walls were generations worth of knowledge from across the continent. The collective wisdom of millions of Amora right at her fingertips. Where she once hit only walls, now she crawled forward.

Isolde's deep brown fingers expertly unrolled a scroll made of delicate parchment. "I think this one has the most potential." Her full lips curled up into an excited smile.

During one of Sara's first visits, Isolde confessed that Amora who came to Sanctum Celestia were often academics doing research. It was rare that she got to help someone solve such a difficult puzzle.

Sara stared at the parchment, her excitement turning into confusion. "I can't read it," she sulked.

"Ahh. My apologies. This is in a dialect from the western side of Arcanos."

"A dialect?" Sara rubbed eyes with her fingertips. She hadn't considered the possibility of the answer being in a language she didn't know.

Isolde placed a hand on Sara's shoulder. "I can read it. You record the translation."

Isolde helped Sara translate the relevant portions of the day's references until the sun was low.

Sara would return a bit after dusk, but her pack was once again filled with hope.

Chapter 21

Bethany

Bethany stood by while Sara set up an offering place under the vibrant red and yellow boughs of a sassafras tree on the east side of their cabin. The warmth of the color did little to heat the cold morning air, and Bethany pulled the knit blanket tighter around her shoulders.

Sara said it was the autumn equinox, and Bethany had to take her word for it because she'd lost track of how long they'd been in the valley. Celebrating felt useless. The feast was a community ritual, and they were far from their community.

Sara's community.
They wanted you dead, remember?

"Exactly," Bethany muttered.

"Exactly what?" Sara asked as she made a pile of young bayberries.

"Why are we doing this?" Bethany sighed, ignoring Sara's question. "This is supposed to be a community celebration, and our community wanted to execute me."

Sara groaned as she eased herself up, using the tree to keep her balance. Bethany's magic struggled to reach the swelling in Sara's knees. It reached out like the woodbine that twisted around the nearby trees, but an invisible wall held the tendrils back.

Blocked.

"The elders failed you and the community," Sara said. "But we do this for the Goddesses who helped us get this far."

Bethany rolled her eyes. She wasn't sure why; she knew Sara was right.

And what good has that done?

"A lot of good that's done," Bethany muttered.

Sara threw her head back with a familiar frustrated sigh.

"I didn't ask you to do this," Bethany spat as she turned around and stomped toward the cabin.

While Sara pored over books and scrolls at Sanctum Celestia, Bethany sat alone in the cabin with her pain, her anger, her guilt, and her thoughts. The mental anguish was often more to bear than the nightmares that kept her from sleeping. She tried to leave once, but she barely made it twenty paces before she was herded back to the door by their red wolf guardians. She considered making a run for it and letting them take her down, but she suspected they'd just protect her where she lay until Sara returned.

Still wrapped in the blanket, Bethany fell into a ratty armchair and extended her feet towards the fire. She refused to let Sara help her with her boots and had gone out wanting to feel the earth on her skin even though it had long stopped replenishing her magic.

You would never leave your daughter or put someone else ahead of her.

You protect her so thoroughly no one knows she exists.

Sara stepped over the threshold with the look of a pissed-off woman determined to start a fight. Bethany didn't let her get the first word in.

"What mother leaves her children for another woman?" Bethany asked.

The question stopped Sara in her tracks. A knife to the stomach would have hurt less than the emotional pain that Bethany just inflicted.

She opened her mouth to apologize but instead she said, "You abandoned your children, and left them without a mother for the foreseeable future. For what? A woman you screw in the woods?"

Bethany tried to take all the words back.

She didn't mean them, and she didn't believe them, but all she could do was watch Sara's beautiful hazel eyes become glassy with tears.

Sara! Please! I don't know why I keep saying these things!

Bethany's silent pleas never reached her lips. She was in a nightmare from which she couldn't shake free.

Without a word, Sara crossed the room to the kitchen and pulled a vial from a shelf. The elixir was the latest in attempts to find an end to Bethany's suffering, but Sara was hesitant to try it because two of the plants were no longer found in the area and she had to substitute them. She didn't know what kind of impact those substitutions would make.

Standing over Bethany, Sara pulled the top. "Take this willingly, or by force. Your choice."

Bethany lifted her arm to take the vial, but she struggled against the same wall that blocked her magic. An invisible resistance that strengthened with each passing day.

Sara's face softened when she noticed the effort. "Can I?"

Bethany nodded and opened her mouth. The liquid slid down Bethany's throat, warming her belly and her chest. Her body loosened and the heaviness in her arm faded. Within moments, she fell asleep.

The cabin was dark and quiet when Bethany woke. She was thirsty and hungry but the pain in her body was minimal.

Bethany wasn't sure where Sara came from, but she tracked her shadowy figure as she placed another log on the fire. The flames grew, illuminating the room. Moving silently, Sara moved out of Bethany's view and returned a few moments later with a bowl of stew.

"I'm sorry," Bethany said, her voice scratchy and weak.

"I know," Sara replied, but there was little warmth in her voice.

Bethany ate a few spoonfuls of stew, letting the food give her the strength to tell Sara everything before she couldn't again.

"I never told you about Adessa. My daughter." Bethany's eyes focused on the meditative motion of stirring her stew. Sara stood somewhere nearby, Bethany could tell that much.

"She's well, as far as I know," Bethany continued. "I didn't leave her. She chose to go with her father to protect the Passage of Souls on the western coast of Arcanos. I used to speak about her often."

Bethany's voice wavered, and she took a few deep, calming breaths. "But just before I came to Belhaven, the elders of Willow Ridge warned that the Commarasi were abducting healers. I use a different family name and no longer speak of her. I've erased her from my life in hopes it would keep her safe."

Bethany chanced a glance at Sara. Her shoulders were hunched forward, her body loose but not relaxed.

"That's the heartbreak you were speaking of that day in Willow Ridge," Sara recalled.

"I don't for a second believe you're a bad mother," Bethany pressed with as much conviction as her voice could muster.

"Those are not my thoughts, and they were not my words. But I am wracked with guilt that you've left your children because I've given up hope that you'll find something that will free me from this fate."

Sara sat on the floor next to Bethany, her gaze trained on the flickering flames.

"What do you mean those are not your words?" Sara asked quietly.

"I hear a voice inside me," Bethany said. She spoke quickly while she still had control of her voice. "It's grown louder. It takes my fears and my worries and twists them into the truth. I'm afraid soon I won't be able to tell the difference between the voice and my own thoughts and desires. Sometimes it speaks for me, like it did this afternoon. It uses my body to utter its lies."

"Did John Dawson speak of a voice?" asked Sara, her tone unreadable.

"Yes. Just before he died, he told me about how the voice verbalized his deepest fears and resentments, destroying his heart and mind while his body withered."

Sara exhaled slowly. Her anger radiated from her body and soaked into Bethany's skin. "Why didn't you tell me this sooner?"

Tears welled in Bethany's eyes, blurring the dancing fire before rolling down her cheeks. "I didn't think it was relevant at first. Hallucinations are common when people are close to the end. I wrote it down in my patient journal, but the council guards confiscated it when they brought me in. And by the time I realized I was hearing the same voice, it had me convinced you wouldn't believe me."

Sara pushed up onto her knees and took Bethany's chilled hands in hers.

"Let me be clear," Sara said. The fire behind her outlined her body in a heavenly glow and for a moment, Bethany thought she was looking at a Goddess sent to earth.

"I'm incredibly pissed off that you kept this information from me, but I will not feed this anger. I love you, and I will fight for you until *our* last breath."

Chapter 22

Sara

A winter-like chill hung in the air and the stars twinkled softly against an indigo sky. Even the crows had yet to wake. The red wolf pups slept nearby in a fluffy pile while their parents and older siblings eyed Sara with curiosity.

The lantern she held cast long shadows against the barn walls where Zephyr slept. Her horse looked up when Sara approached, the mare's groggy eyes dark pools of black.

"I know it's early," Sara said as she collected her riding gear. "But I don't think Bethany is sick. I think there's something inside her. So we have to make one more journey to Sanctum Celestia. And then you can sleep as late as you like."

Zephyr chuffed and begrudgingly eased herself up.

As Sara mounted the mare, the smallest of her corvid guides landed nearby. He would have blended into the shadows if not for the peculiar markings of white feathers. He examined a silver button Sara left on the windowsill as an offering of appreciation for their constant protection.

"Are you my escort this morning?"

The crow bobbed its head and took flight, Sara and Zephyr following after.

The darkness slowed the already grueling ride, and Sara's impatience was fueled by physical and emotional exhaustion. The dawn sun was still hidden behind the thick tree canopy when Sara passed under Sanctum Celestia's stone archway.

Isolde stood at the entrance, and it was the first time Sara had seen the woman outside the library's walls. A fur pelt was wrapped around her shoulders, and instead of her librarian cloak, she wore simple trousers and a heavy tunic. On any other day, the unusual meeting would have struck Sara as something of concern, but Bethany was her only focus.

"Isolde! I think I have the key to solving our mystery!" Sara spoke quickly as she jumped off her horse and scrambled to the door. "Bethany is hearing voices that control her thoughts and her body. I only learned this last night, but I think it's exactly what we need to narrow our search."

Isolde stood firm and tall in front of the door, blocking Sara from entering the library. "They sent warning of you."

"What? Who?" Sara sputtered, her greatest fear coming true.

"The Council of Nine on the Isle of Belhaven sent a warning across Valen that a dangerous prisoner escaped, aided by an herbal alchemist intent on curing what cannot be healed."

Sara searched Isolde's face. Her voice held a chill of seriousness, but her hazel eyes remained warm and sympathetic. She'd been more than kind and compassionate, but Sara's emotions couldn't be contained any longer.

"They were going to murder her, Isolde! Did they include that in their warning? Contracting an illness—or whatever this is—isn't a crime and yet they sentenced her to a cleansing execution. No one even thought to send me here, to this library, until we escaped. I will not let her die until I have tried everything in this realm and others to keep her alive!"

Isolde remained silent but something changed in the librarian's features. Almost like realization or an idea. Whatever it was, it was gone as quickly as it came, and Sara feared her outburst may have signaled the guards. She slowly placed a hand on the hilt of the dagger strapped to her hip. She wouldn't hurt anyone, but she would defend herself so that she could return to Bethany, even empty-handed.

"We are entering into a very fragile time, my dear," said Isolde. "Those we love may have to be sacrificed to maintain our ways."

The suggestion that Bethany would have to be sacrificed for some greater good filled Sara with a rage so hot that tears streamed down her cheeks. Sara opened her mouth, but Isolde spoke again before Sara could plead her case.

"Even if I wanted to help you and your beloved, I have no way of doing so. I believe you will need a spell that comes from Teremedi found in the *Cipher of Stellara.*"

Isolde's voice kept its harshness, but the urging in her eyes begged for Sara's focus.

"The *Cipher* is protected in the lowest vault of this sanctuary," Isolde continued. "Only those it deems worthy may access it. I am unable to descend into that part of the library, and I assure you, I'm unworthy."

Isolde paused, giving Sara time to process everything she had just heard. She committed to memory every bit of Isolde's detailed instructions.

"Rest as long as you like before your journey home, but I *will not* speak to you again should your elders question if you walked through my halls."

Sara bowed her head as Isolde walked past her towards the gardens, leaving the entrance unguarded.

Sara looked up at the morning sky, now a watercolor painting of deep pink and glowing orange. "Thank you," she whispered.

Sara walked swiftly to the back of the grand temple, then jogged along the perimeter until she found a staircase hidden deep within its corners. Only a few torches lit the steep stone steps that descended into the temple's lowest levels. Every step was taken with a divine force pulling her forward.

At the end of her journey, a pearlescent leather-bound book was displayed on an altar in the center of an otherwise empty rotunda. The stale air buzzed with lethal magic, and Sara's own vibrated in reply. It was less of a warning and more of a threat. Etched into the stone were ancient carvings of the Amora, the deities that founded their culture and shared their magic with humans.

Without considering the consequences of her impulses, Sara stepped through the archway leading into the sacred space. The protection spell burned her skin like a swarm of bees. Sara refused to scream as her soul was judged by the invisible fire, but released a primal cry when she emerged within arm's reach of the sacred book.

Sara didn't spare a moment to reflect on what it meant to be deemed worthy of wielding the most powerful of Amora magic. She grabbed the *Cipher*, hugged it to her chest, and ran.

She ran through the tunnels and up the steep stone steps into the library. Her lungs burned, but she didn't stop until she reached Zephyr, then begged the Goddesses to get them home quickly and safely.

Once in the familiarity of the forest around the cabin, Sara's bottled emotions began bubbling to the surface. She slowed Zephyr to a stop and dismounted.

She collapsed to her knees and cried tears of relief.

Tears of joy.

Tears of frustration.

Tears of fear.

She finally had the key to saving Bethany.

CHAPTER 23
LETTER HOME

I write you this letter with true hope in my soul. I've uncovered the source of Bethany's suffering and while it is far worse than I imagined, there is a way to save her.

Bethany is the mortal host to an Orostori demon. They move freely in Teremedi but require a mortal body should they wish to walk among us in Tereprima. Centuries ago, the Orostori would lure Amora through the rift and possess their first victim. Once they are in our realm, they seek new hosts, becoming stronger with every possession.

With our brave gatekeepers minding the rifts across Arcanos, we haven't seen their kind in several generations.

In this letter, I'm including my notes on the Orostori so that you may share this information with our council and the elders of nearby villages. It is imperative that the gates to Teremedi are not left unprotected.

I have all the ingredients needed to perform the spell, but the vessel of iron has been much harder to acquire without giving myself away. I'm in a small village attempting to procure one and taking the opportunity to send you this message.

I will be performing the spell in a few days during the next full moon. I will do my best to reach out to you again to confirm my success.

I love all of you with every fiber of my heart and soul.

Sara

Orostori Demon

An often-malevolent spirit with moderate power that moves freely within Teremedi.

Has <u>no corporal body</u> of its own and cannot survive long in Tereprima without a mortal host.

<u>PARASITIC</u> >>> Feeds on the spirit and life force of its host. Prefers sadness, anger, and fear. Will control its host's thoughts to create the environment on which it feeds.

It can control a host's thoughts, words, and actions. ITS FINAL FORM WILL ALLOW IT TO CONTROL A HOST WITHOUT KILLING THEM.

When the host is weak, the demon will seek out another host and force a transfer.

<u>DEATH OF THE PREVIOUS HOST IS LIKELY.</u>

Demon is weak after its transfer but grows stronger with each host.

Should the host perish before another suitable host is found >>> <u>Orostori will invade the nearest mortal.</u>

Without a host, it will return to Teremedi. It is believed that the <u>Orostori retains its host's memories.</u>

Expulsion spell

A soulmate of the host MUST perform the spell. SOULMATE MAGIC REQUIRED TO EXPEL AND TRAP TO PREVENT REINFECTION.

Can be trapped in iron vessel made by Amora metalworker.

DESTRUCTION REQUIRES THE STRENGTH OF BONDED MAGIC BETWEEN HOST AND SPELLCASTER.

Risk

DEATH

Host and mage must have compatible magic

CHAPTER 24
SARA

Sara wrapped a blanket around herself and stepped outside into the cold night. The full moon climbed a starless sky, illuminating the forest in an ethereal glow.

The red wolves were closer than usual, but still at a safe distance.

"Everything will be okay soon," she said to them, but also to herself.

Sara ran her fingers over her necklace, the gemstones warm from the heat of her chest trapped by the blanket. She blindly followed the sharp edges and smooth planes of quartz and sandstone, and the twists and turns of the wire that held them all together.

Bethany's health had plummeted in the month since Sara stole the *Cipher of Stellara*. As Bethany's physical body deteriorated, the Orostori demon's hold on her mind grew stronger. Sara assisted Bethany with her most basic human needs every day while the demon inside her spoke vitriolic lies.

They dealt with the same sort of abuse from John, but his words lacked the intimacy of Bethany's. John and Sara were friends, but not the kind that would confide in each other. Bethany knew so much about Sara, including her vulnerabilities, and the demon used those with fervor.

Sara walked around the cabin to a hollow tree basking in the moonlight. She tapped her fingers on the trunk a few times and when nothing skittered from the void, she reached inside, pulling out the *Cipher*, the iron urn, and the glass vial filled with the sweet-smelling liquid she'd mixed the night before. Only one final ingredient was left to add.

Taking another deep breath of the autumn air, Sara asked the Goddesses for their protection and headed back inside.

It was time.

"Oh you've returned! I thought you left me again," Bethany called from the bed in the corner of the room. There was no missing the insincerity in her tone. "Like you left your family."

Sara took no joy in traveling to Covendale in search of the iron vessel the spell required. She had no way of knowing how long the quest would take or if she'd be successful. She was, but Sara was forced to wait until nightfall to pilfer the container from the village metalworker, and her escape in the darkness only prolonged her return.

"And I returned to you, just like I will to my family," Sara replied cooly.

Sara stole a glance at her. Bethany lay prone with one arm hanging limp off the side of the bed. Sara had braided Bethany's thinning hair and covered it with a scarf that was starting to slide to one side. Sara longed for the return of the vibrant green of Bethany's eyes, which were now voids of black.

Bethany's plump figure disappeared, leaving a flesh-covered skeleton. With already so little for them to eat, Sara sometimes worried that Bethany wouldn't last the winter even if she survived the banishment of the demon. She returned to her task when the demon began to taunt her.

Sara considered sedating Bethany just for the quiet, but she wasn't certain anything would work at this point. Humming an old lullaby, Sara entered a hypnotic state that kept her focus on the task instead of the increasingly vulgar obscenities being lobbed at her.

Sara poured a clear, aromatic liquid into a bowl and used a clean cloth to soak her skin. The earthy scents of yarrow, witch hazel, and yellowroot floated into the air with every brush. The cleansing water mixed with her magic and warmed her body from the outside in, then it cooled, leaving the freshness of a mountain spring. When she finished, she set the bowl aside and picked up a jar of ointment. She smoothed a generous amount on the insides of her wrists and temples. She held her necklace in one hand while spreading the ointment on her chest.

She shook out her arms and bounced on her toes to diffuse some of the nervous energy. Sara was confident the spell would work if she performed it correctly. The key to its success was a mutual love between the caster and the victim, and the necklace that hung around Sara's neck was a tangible symbol of what they shared. Bethany's love was infused within the crystals and like the pull of their magic, it was impossible to ignore.

But saving Bethany would be emotionally and physically painful for them both, and the primal part of her brain—and her magic—wanted to avoid that harm at all costs.

A harsh caw from somewhere in the room startled Sara out of her hesitation. The small crow with the unusual white wings hadn't left Sara's side since the day he escorted her to Sanctum Celestia.

Sara couldn't delay any longer.

The ritual to expel the Orostori demon from Bethany's body needed to be performed during a short window of time at the height of the full moon. If Sara missed it, neither of them would be returning to Belhaven.

She picked up a basket of rope near the door and brought it to Bethany's bedside.

"Oh you smell divine, my love," Bethany drawled, flopping over onto her back. "Are those cleansing herbs on your skin? You must be getting ready for some big magic."

"Very big magic, Bethy. And I need you to be still while I do it."

Bethany erupted in maniacal laughter, and Sara wasn't sure what to make of it. It was so unlike her. But she knew Bethany was still in there somewhere, fighting for freedom.

Distracted, Sara almost missed Bethany's open hand heading for her cheek. She covered her face just in time to deflect the blow. She was less surprised that Bethany tried to smack her and more surprised that she had the strength to attempt it with such force.

Bethany swung again, but Sara caught her arm this time. Bethany had become so frail that Sara's fingertips touched when they wrapped around her wrist. She screamed and thrashed against Sara's hold, swinging at Sara with her free hand. Sara thanked the Goddesses that she had the foresight to prepare the binds beforehand. She slipped one loop around Bethany's wrist and yanked her arm over her head and through the bedpost. She grabbed Bethany's other wrist and slipped it into the second loop, securing both of Bethany's arms over her head.

"Usually a girl has to pay to have this kind of fun," Bethany cooed.

Sara almost laughed because that was something Bethany would say. But fleeting moments where it sounded like Bethany was breaking through was how the Orostori tricked Sara into letting her guard down.

"We'll do this as much as you want after I get this fucking demon out of you."

"Oh is that what's going on here?"

Sara fought to secure Bethany's kicking feet.

"That spell is incredibly precise. One small mistake, and you'll both die."

"Yes, well," Sara said through gritted teeth as she tightened the binds around Bethany's ankles. "At least you'll go back to where you belong. Floating around Teremedi, whining about not having a body."

It laughed Bethany's laugh.

"You mortals are so busy fighting amongst yourselves," it sneered. "I'll be back in another body well before yours turns to dust."

"That may be true, but I left instructions so hopefully your next stay is a short one."

Leaving Bethany's side, Sara crossed the room to the table where the *Cipher* sat with the tools needed for the ritual. She uncorked the vial and poured the liquid into a heavy black tourmaline bowl.

Sara pulled her dagger from the sheath and held the blade over the fire. An orange glow danced in the smokey crystals embedded in the hilt while the flames licked the steel.

When she pulled it from the fire, she plunged the blade into the same water she used to purify her body, cleansing and cooling the metal.

"Is such spectacle necessary?" Demon Bethany asked. "Amora are so dramatic with their rituals."

Sara stared into the dark orbs of Bethany's demon eyes and sliced her finger open, allowing a bubble of blood to pool at the tip. Sara let several drops fall into the bowl before picking it up and walking to the north wall of the cabin.

"Like I said, dramatic," Demon Bethany scoffed.

Sara dipped her bloodied finger into the bowl and stirred it until it was coated in the mixture. She dragged her finger over the wood and stone wall until a crude symbol appeared. Then she drew two more.

She repeated the markings on each wall all the while trying her best to block out the incessant chatter of the demon in the corner of the room. She knew it was trying to distract her. The moon was almost at its zenith, and the ritual was precise. The demon was too weak to overtake her physically, but it could buy itself some time.

Sara wouldn't let it.

Three more markings went on the side of the iron urn.

Growing desperate, the demon fought against the bindings, shaking the rickety bed frame.

"Who's going to tell your family that you're dead, Sara? You promised them you'd be back, but you won't. You'll perform this spell poorly, it won't work, and if the magic doesn't kill you, I will. And I'll use Bethany's hands to do it."

Sara had long reached her breaking point, but she forced herself to remain calm so as to not make a mistake. Sara climbed onto the bed and straddled Bethany's hips, pressing her knees tight to keep them steady.

"I'm so sorry for this, Bethy." Sara tore open Bethany's tunic, exposing the other woman's emaciated chest. She said a silent apology as she drew three marks below Bethany's collarbone, her skin still cold as ice.

"This isn't over. You think that teapot can contain me?"

Without a breath of hesitation, she drew the dagger from her hip, sliced open her palm, and poured the remnants of the vial over the wound.

"I'll get out and find your descendants and end their lives and your family line."

Sara laughed. "Now who's being dramatic?"

Sara covered Bethany's mouth with her bloody palm, holding tight as the body under her tried to shake her off.

Gusts of icy wind came from nowhere and everywhere, filling the cabin and circling so quickly things began to move toward the center of its pull. Bethany stopped fighting and went limp. The Orostori swirled around the room as a wailing mist of wrath and despair.

Sara wrapped her arms around Bethany's small body, pulling her in tight and whispering vows of love and happiness. The pull of the icy wind strengthened as it was sucked inside the urn. It sucked the air from Sara's lungs and the glow from the fire.

Then it stopped.

Embers in the fireplace roared back to life and the heat returned. The top of the urn had been sealed shut, and the container sat motionless in the center of the room.

"Thank fuck that thing is gone," Bethany mumbled against Sara's chest.

Sara's relieved laugh turned into a sob as warmth spread from their touching skin. She pulled away just enough to see Bethany smile weakly. Then kissed Bethany's warm lips as their tears fell and mixed in salty pools. Sara used her thumbs to wipe Bethany's cheeks and bathed in the heat that had been gone far too long.

Epilogue

Isle of Belhaven, one year later

Bethany stood still and silent at the entrance to the catacombs under Belhaven's Amora temple. Her heart pounded against her tightening chest. She hadn't been back there since Piper and Ophelia freed her from its dank prison.

Her mind remembered little from her time banished by the village's former elders.

But her body remembered.

Her magic remembered.

Sara had gone ahead with Ophelia to ensure the path was safe. Devastating winter storms hit the continent with a force few had seen. Much of Belhaven was destroyed by wind, heavy snow, or flooding from the sea. Sara and Bethany barely survived in their small cabin, and when they returned to Belhaven almost a year later, it was to a place that looked dramatically different but felt more like home.

A gentle hand took her own and squeezed it three times. I. Love. You.

Bethany closed her eyes and sucked in the cool, damp air. She let it out slowly and opened her eyes to see Lenni standing beside her.

"You can do this," she said softly. "But if you don't want to, I'll stay with you."

Bethany squeezed Lenni's hand three times in response as a few tears escaped down her cheek.

"No, let's go," Bethany said, beginning to worry that Sara was in danger and couldn't come back. "Let's meet up with Mama."

Step after step they descended into the catacombs, following the winding path and earthen walls lined with art. Where there was destruction above, there was peace down below. It eased Bethany's anxiety just a bit, and when her magic tangled with Sara's, she released a long sigh of relief.

Sara and Ophelia came into view. Their shadows dancing wildly in the firelight of their lanterns.

Ophelia and Sara each had one end of a wooden chest, and Sara braced herself as the other woman counted off. They heaved the trunk into one of the empty spaces in the wall, shoving it back as far as it could go.

"That doesn't look too steady," Lenni said.

"I agree," said Ophelia observing the edge of the chest that hung out over the wall. "But water is a bigger risk than falling. I'll come back tomorrow with some wood to brace it."

"What if someone comes down here and finds it?" Lenni asked.

"Ophelia is using her light magic to hide it in the shadows," Sara said.

Lenni narrowed her eyes and pressed her lips to one side. Bethany could tell her thoughtful daughter was skeptical, and she couldn't blame the child. The magic would begin to fade after Ophelia's death unless another luminary recast and held the spell.

Bethany put an arm around Lenni, wanting to return the comfort her new daughter had given her.

"None of this is ideal," Bethany said. "The important thing now is keeping it out of the hands of the Commarasi. Hopefully our calls for a pair of bound souls will be answered and we can destroy this demon."

"How many pairs of bound souls are there?" Lenni asked. "Are they common like soulmates?"

Sara, Bethany, and Ophelia exchanged a look, none quite sure how best to answer the question while easing her worries. Bound souls were thought to be rare, but with so many Amora spread throughout Arcanos, there was no way of knowing. Bethany's best guess would be a few pairs in each generation.

"Not like soulmates, Len," Sara finally said, brushing a strand of hair away from her daughter's forehead. "They're quite rare. But when they come together, the power of their magic is unmatched."

Acknowledgements

To the beautiful soul that picked up *Bound by Ink* and kept reading until the end, thank you. There are millions of books in the world and I am honored that you chose to spend your time with one of mine.

Love and gratitude to my critique partners (the MILFs) for being Sara and Bethany's biggest fans and to my beta readers who helped me take a mess of a manuscript and turn it into gold.

To Ruthie Bowles for your insight, your experience, and your labor. I appreciate you and I'm so excited for what's to come.

Jenny Sliger really earned her paycheck with this one. I'm grateful for every appropriate comma placement and your time spent going on entomology deep dives.

Amanda Hawkins has outdone herself once again, giving me a cover that I'm ready to make my entire personality.

To my friends who shamelessly recommend my book and celebrate my wins, I adore you.

To my parents for their unwavering support. I'm here because of you.

To Chuck and Killian, I love you both with every fiber of my heart and soul. Thank you for taking this journey with me.

About Ariella

Ariella is a former journalist, but uses "former" loosely. Her curiosity for all things is insatiable and research is her favorite part of any project.She writes cozy contemporary and high stakes fantasy romances. Her work is swoony and open door and absolutely not intended for readers who are under 18.

Someone once told her to write what you know so all her millennial protagonists are bisexual, neurodivergent, and live with chronic mental illness. They mostly have their shit together and Ariella chronicles their coming-of-middle-age stories.

When she's not writing, she teaches yoga and falls behind on laundry. She lives in the suburbs of Raleigh, North Carolina with her husband, child, a collection of aging pets, and a flock of chickens that won't stop tearing up the new plants in her flower garden.

Visit my website to read my blog or buy your next book.

Subscribe to my newsletter for book updates and bonus content.

More books by Ariella

Contemporary Romance

Let it Rain
Radio Romance
Chasing Ember

Fantasy Romance

Roots in Ink, Scions of Belhaven, Book 1
Bound by Ink, Scions of Belhaven Novella

SWEET MAGNOLIA SHOP

signed paperbacks
special editions
ebooks you own

ariellamonti.com/shop

Belhaven Island

Circa 2017

Mabel Turner didn't stop the tears that rolled down her cheeks and landed on the crumpled sheet of paper in her hands. She'd been carrying it around for weeks, stuffed in her pocket or her purse because any time she set the letter down, she expected it to vanish, taking with it the long-sought information.

The gentle breeze off Belhaven Sound dried her cheeks, leaving her skin stiff with a dusting of salt. The floating dock where she sat swayed with the familiar rhythm of a visitor's footfalls. She wiped her eyes and her face with an embroidered handkerchief she kept stuffed in her jacket pocket.

"I'm surprised this hunk of wood isn't at the bottom of the ocean," said the visitor, her voice raspy from a lifetime of smoking.

Mabel laughed in agreement. She wasn't sure what was keeping the old dock together. It certainly wasn't magic. The woodworker who built it was long gone. The dock was probably one of the few things that remained from a time when Belhaven's Amora could freely practice magic.

Siena DiMarco eased herself onto the iron bench next to Mabel, setting aside an ornate walking stick that Mabel recognized as once belonging to Siena's mother, Rose.

Mabel fidgeted in her seat. She couldn't remember the last time Siena DiMarco's magic had connected with hers, seeking it out like sunflowers seek the sun. Their magic melted together, forming something perfectly unique. Perfectly complete.

And it was for those reasons that it made Mabel particularly sad.

The two women sat in silence as the seagulls circled above, diving towards the water when a fish entered their sights.

Siena spoke first. "You said you needed my help."

Her voice was gentle but impatient. Mabel didn't take it personally, though. Siena had been like this for as long as Mabel could remember. Siena walked through the world like she didn't have time to savor the quiet moments. There was a time in their lives when Siena would say the Goddesses matched her with Mabel as a much-needed counterbalance.

Like the woodworker, those days were long gone.

"I need someone pulled out of The Forge," Mabel said, looking towards the western horizon.

Siena sucked in a breath and turned in her seat. Mabel felt her shocked stare on her skin.

"That's a big ask," Siena said. "Who?"

Mabel held out the tear-stained page. It was still too hard to look Siena in the eye. "Cara."

Siena took it from her, and Mabel heard the rustle of Siena fumbling with her reading glasses. "Your niece has been there this whole time? Why didn't you tell me?"

Mabel huffed a laugh, annoyed with the implication that she would withhold information. "I wasn't sure what happened to her after my sister and brother-in-law got swept up in the last raid on the compound. I had to pull a lot of favors to get this confirmation."

Siena folded the page in quarters and pulled a lighter from a pocket inside her jacket. She held one corner over the flames until the paper caught. Mabel watched the fire dance dangerously close to Siena's pale, arthritic fingers. When she couldn't hold it any longer, Siena dropped the remains into the water below.

She protected that piece of paper with her life, and now it was nothing but ash mixing with the sea.

"I'm calling in one more," Mabel said, finally making eye contact with her oldest friend and longest love. Siena's features had aged, and her brown hair grayed, but the fire in her hazel eyes remained the same.

"You're the only one I trust to bring her here."

"Fuck, Mabel. She's a healer for Elijah Alden. I don't know if we have the resources for that."

Mabel narrowed her eyes and with a slight tilt of her head said, "I don't remember you considering my or Rose's resources every time you left Emma in our care."

Siena's eyes widened with a flash of anger that quickly dissipated into something like shame.

This time, Siena looked away. "How is Emma?"

"Good." Mabel turned back toward the water in time to see a loon pop up from the water with a silvery fish. "She's an excellent storyteller. It's fascinating how she toes the line with the museum exhibits."

A smile ghosted over Siena's face. "Is she still practicing?"

"As much as any of us can," Mabel said with a sigh. "She'd be doing better if she heard from her mother more often."

Mabel knew where the comment would ultimately take them. Their time together was rare, and she didn't want to spend it being so antagonistic, but maybe this time it'd be worth it.

Siena scoffed and rolled her eyes, but Mabel knew her well enough to recognize fake emotions.

"I think Emma has enough to deal with even when I'm not around."

Mabel wasn't ignorant of the hardships Emma dealt with being Siena DiMarco's daughter. Carrying a family history of Amora resistance against the Commarasi made Emma a target of bullying as a child and increased surveillance as an adult. It impacted her career and her relationships. In Siena's mind, the less time Emma spent with the surviving DiMarco matriarch, the better.

"You could at least try being honest about why you keep her at a distance," Mabel urged gently.

Siena sighed loudly with aggravation, and Mabel almost laughed at how much it sounded like Emma's.

"Great idea. I could start with telling her that I'm the person you come to when you want help extracting a niece you never told her about from the headquarters of a government-sanctioned criminal organization."

"Point made, SiSi." Mabel put her hands up as a show of surrender.

"I haven't heard you call me SiSi in a long time." The gentleness returned to Siena's voice, and a wistfulness replaced the impatience. "I'll see what we can manage. It'll take a while to plan, and there won't be much notice once executed, so be prepared."

Mabel reached for her hand, interlocking their fingers, wrinkled and stiff with age, but somehow still two pieces of the same puzzle. "Thank you," she whispered.

Siena nodded but didn't let go.

Need More?

Did you read the bonus scene yet?

Subscribe to my newsletter for access to a bonus scene where Liam and Emma drop some clues for the setting of the second full novel in the Scions of Belhaven series.

Scan the QR code or follow the Bookfunnel link for access.

Current subscribers can also find the link at the bottom of each newsletter.

dl.bookfunnel.com
/3f5yxfzlt6